THE LAST DANCE

THE SOUL SURVIVOR SERIES:

The Mind Siege Project
All the Rave

THE LAST DANCE

TIM LaHAYE
AND BOB DeMOSS

W PUBLISHING GROUP™

www.wpublishinggroup.com

A Division of Thomas Nelson, Inc.
www.ThomasNelson.com

Copyright © 2002 by Tim LaHaye and Bob DeMoss

Published by W Publishing Group, Nashville, Tennessee, in association with the literary agency of Alive Communications, Inc., 7680 Goddard Street, Suite 200, Colorado Springs, CO 80920.

Scripture quotations used in this book are from the Holy Bible, New International Version (NIV). Copyright © 1973, 1978, 1984, International Bible Society. Used by permission of Zondervan Bible Publishers.

This is a work of fiction. Names, characters, places, and incidents either are the product of the authors' imaginations or are used fictitiously. Any resemblance to actual persons, living or dead, events, organizations, or locales is entirely coincidental and beyond the intent of the authors or publisher.

ISBN 0-8499-4321-3

Printed in the United States of America

02 03 04 05 06 PHX 6 5 4 3 2 1

To Marty and Ruth Ozinga
For your loving support over the years

PROLOGUE

It was Tuesday night, and the Philadelphia Memorial Public Library closed in fifteen minutes. The array of five iMac computers arranged on a large wooden table sat idle. At precisely 9:45, a man with a knapsack in his right hand entered the old, brick library. He passed by the checkout desk, careful to avoid eye contact with the librarian, and then made his way to the computer station at the rear of the facility.

He took his usual spot behind the iMac that faced away from public scrutiny. He placed his bag on the floor at his feet. He cracked his knuckles and then logged on to the Internet, thankful that the head librarian refused to install filtering software. The glow of the computer screen cast a pale, bluish white light on his unshaven face as he worked.

Seconds later, he opened his knapsack, retrieved a zip disk, and jammed it into the mouth of the computer, which—just his luck—had been specially modified by the library to accommodate zip disks. Within a minute the compressed contents of its 100-megabyte capacity were uploaded to his Web site.

As he worked, a voice from the overhead intercom softly informed all patrons to make their final selections and proceed to the checkout. The library would close in seven minutes. He checked his watch. No problem. He needed just five minutes more.

He continued his routine in silence, his fingers dancing across the keyboard with purpose. The transfer of data from the disk to the Web now complete, he initiated a reverse transfer of financial information to the zip. A smile eased across his face as he reviewed the last in a long string of numbers.

One million dollars.

His eyes narrowed as he stared at the number. With his damp left hand he stroked his chin for a long minute before logging off. He removed the zip disk and placed it in his bag, then retrieved a towel and a small spray bottle from a side pocket. He sprayed a gentle mist of the special solution onto the towel and then wiped off the keyboard and the body of the computer where he had inserted the zip disk. Satisfied, he replaced the items in the knapsack.

As he stood to leave, he caught a glimpse of the clock on the wall: 9:58. He flung the knapsack over one shoulder and then took his time as he walked past the stacks of reference materials, careful not to touch anything as he departed. When the librarian offered a good night, he managed a grunt—and no eye contact.

Outside the library, the cool evening air filled his lungs. He inhaled deeply as he lingered at the top of the concrete steps that led down to the parking lot. He began to descend the dozen steps, but stopped when his cell phone played a distinct melody. He had specifically assigned this tune to help him identify the caller before he answered it.

Although he half expected the call, his heart still jumped. His nerves always seemed to be on heightened sensitivity during his trips to the library. He glanced around to ensure his conversation wouldn't be heard before answering. "Yo."

"What's the good word?"

He gripped the phone and spoke just above a whisper. "We just hit the magic number: fifty thousand subscribers. Hold on . . ." He looked over his shoulder as two teens left the building. He waited for them to pass. "At twenty bucks a pop, that's—what?—a million bucks. Gotta love it, right?" He could hear a whistle on the other end of the line.

"You da man," the voice said. "Come see me as soon as you can. Maybe tomorrow, okay?"

"I'll try. Hang in there, bro." That said, he folded up his phone with a snap, stuffed it into his front jean pocket, and then headed to his vehicle.

eather, you can't be serious." Jodi Adams wiped her fingers on a napkin as she spoke. "You actually turned Stan down? I mean, this is the prom we're talking about. And you've always said he's so—you know—hot!"

Heather Barnes shrugged off her best friend's assessment. "And why is my decision such a big deal?" Heather reached for another fry. "Stan's a big boy. He'll find someone else. Come to think of it, why don't you go with him, Kat? I saw the way you two were hanging out—"

"Right." Kat Koffman rolled her eyes. "As if I'm just gonna ask him. Don't get me wrong; if he asked me I'd go in a heartbeat."

"I still say you should reconsider, Heather," Jodi said.

"Don't hate me," said Kat, chewing on a wad of gum as she sat between Jodi and Heather, "but I think I'm, like, with Jodi on this. I mean, most girls—"

"I know, I know." Heather waved her off. She scrunched her nose before adding, ". . . most girls would just d-i-e to go with Stan 'da Man' to the prom."

The trio sat closely in the corner booth of Johnny Angel's, a '50s retro diner considered the absolute best place to get a shake, burger, and fries. The girls had almost depleted a boat of chili-cheese fries while waiting for their meal.

"Besides," Heather added, her eyes drifting down toward the black-and-white-checkered floor, "if he cared so much, why'd he wait until the very last minute to ask me?" She looked up at Jodi. "I mean, the prom is in—what?—two days, and he only asked this morning?"

"Hold on," Kat said. "Like, let me get this straight. Some girls would do anything to be asked to the prom *at all*. You get asked by a 100 percent, USDA-grade he-man and you turn him down—because he waited until the week of the prom? I just don't get it." Kat shook her head.

"Even if I wanted to go with him," Heather said, "I've already said yes to someone else."

The alarm on Kat's watch launched into a nagging beep. "Time out, everybody." She made a *T*-sign with her hands. "Gotta take another horse tablet, or your kidney's gonna throw a tantrum, Jodi."

"Wrong-O. *Your* body's the one with rejection issues," Jodi said, smiling. A couple of months earlier Jodi had donated one of her kidneys to Kat, who was involved in a life-threatening accident during a boating trip. But several days ago, Kat's body began to reject the kidney. She might have died at a party if not for the help of Jodi and Bruce Arnold, a mutual friend from school.

Kat swallowed hard as she downed the medicine with a glass of water. "But thank God for these pills, right? So where were we?"

"How Heather dissed Stan," Jodi said smartly.

"Whatever." Heather threw a crumpled napkin at Jodi.

"Come on, Heather, we've been friends forever, right?" Jodi asked. "So, what gives? Why'd you snub him?"

"First of all, I didn't snub him," Heather said. She peeled the paper from her straw before stuffing it into her strawberry shake. "I just don't like putting myself in a situation with someone who has a bad reputation, that's all. I figured you'd understand that much."

"Hey, I'm kinda new at this whole Christianity thing, right?" Kat chimed in. "So help me out here. Why is it a major sin or whatever to go with Stan, anyway?" She looked in Heather's direction.

Heather knew Kat had invited Jesus into her heart a week ago. She smiled. "I . . . see . . . let's just say that I think Stan's a great guy," Heather started. "And I'm not saying it would be a sin to go with him, or anything like that. He can be a blast to hang out with—"

"Don't we know," Kat cut in with a wink.

"Anyway, it's just that he's got certain, um, *expectations*." She paused to see if Kat followed her drift, but was met with a blank expression. "*Physical* expectations," Heather added.

"Oh, now I get it," Kat said, nodding.

"Listen, Kat, I'm not some holier-than-thou type," Heather said, raking her hand through her blond hair. "But, there are some people who might not understand, you know? Besides, like I said, I've got other plans."

"Got it," Kat said. "Boy, do I have a lot to learn." Kat reached for the salt shaker. "How about you, Jodi? Are you going?"

"Nah." Jodi hooked her hair behind her right ear. "And I'm totally cool with that, trust me. I mean, picture me dancing with a couple of bruised ribs." She winced as her right side throbbed at the thought.

For Jodi, it had started ten days ago at an all-night dance party in south Philadelphia. She had changed her mind to go at the last minute, joining Kat, Heather, Bruce, and Stan "da Man" Taylor, the star of the football team. In the end, Jodi found herself running for her life after stumbling upon the dark truth behind the men who sponsored the event. The nightmare ended with a bang when her car crashed into the side of a building, fracturing several ribs. The doctor explained that it would take her several months to heal. She was cautioned to take it easy in the meantime.

Jodi's memories were interrupted when a waitress, juggling three oversized plates, appeared at the edge of the table. "Who's got the burger and onion rings?"

"That'd be me," Kat said, reaching for the plate. Her bangle bracelets jangled as she moved.

"Cheese steak?"

"Right here," Heather directed, clearing a space for the dish.

"Guess the salad's for you, dear," the waitress said, dropping the plate in front of Jodi with a thunk.

"Thank you." Jodi suppressed a laugh.

"Yous guys need anything else, just holler, okay?" She turned and left before anyone could respond.

"So, Heather," Kat said as she baptized her hamburger with catsup, "what's with this mystery date I've been hearing about?"

Jodi noticed that Heather looked away for a split second before answering.

"Um, yeah, I'm going with him," Heather said. "Kinda goes with the territory, seeing as I'm on the Student Senate and all."

"Hey, maybe you know this, Heather," Jodi began, trying to draw her out. "Why is the prom so late this year? I mean, it's almost the middle of June."

Heather took a bite from her sandwich and nodded as she chewed. "The gym floor, remember?" She mumbled the words with her mouth still full.

"What about it?" Jodi asked.

Heather swallowed. "They had to repair it after the ceiling leaked," she said, "but there was a delay or something with the wood tiles so we had to, like, postpone the prom until now. We tried to move it to a different location but everything was already booked."

"Right, but what about Mr. Wonderful? Who is he?" Kat's earrings clinked as she tilted her head.

Heather took another bite. When she finished chewing, she said, "Well, he's a senior at Villanova High—"

"Ooh, a rich kid," Kat joked with a friendly smile.

"Maybe. Okay—probably," Heather said. "But that isn't important. What matters is that he's about the most sensitive, understanding guy I know."

Jodi threw her a skeptical look.

"He is," Heather said. "Like, whenever my parents are on my case— or I have a really bad day—he just seems to know how to lift my spirits. Remember that day when I was home sick? You know, like, last week?"

Jodi and Kat nodded.

"Well, he said if it were up to him, he'd come over to my house and make me a bowl of chicken noodle soup." A faraway look floated across Heather's eyes. "Wasn't that so sweet? He always says stuff like that, especially when I've been down. Guess you could say he makes me feel special, you know?"

Jodi dabbed at the corners of her mouth with her napkin. She felt like gagging, but restrained herself. "So what's his name, or do we need to beat it out of you?"

"John Knox." Heather smiled softly as she spoke his name.

Jodi and Kat were quick to pounce with their questions.

"Where'd you meet him?"

"What's he look like?"

"Is he a jock?"

"When do we meet him?"

"Hey, what is this?" Heather protested. "Twenty Questions?"

Jodi leaned toward Kat's ear and said, "Man, she's got it bad." They shared a laugh.

"Ooh! And she's all top secret about him, too," Kat said while giving Heather a friendly elbow.

"Cut it out, guys." Heather put down her sandwich and folded her slender arms. "Actually, we met in a *Christian* chat room, if you must know. He's eighteen and he's—"

"In a chat room?" Jodi said. Her right eyebrow shot up. "You never told me this part. So, like, when was this?"

"I don't know. Maybe two or three months ago. Why? What's the big deal?" Heather said, shifting in her seat. "We've been talking online almost every night. Oh, and I've got his picture right here in my purse—"

"Wait a second." Jodi put down her fork as a new thought crossed her mind. "Have you ever actually met this guy? I mean, like, in person?"

Heather looked down at her plate and poked at a fry. Jodi could almost hear the silence pass between them.

"Oh my gosh," Kat said, bringing a hand to her mouth. "You must be kidding. You've never met John—and you're going to go to the prom with him? That's nuts!"

"I knew you guys wouldn't understand," Heather said.

Kat cut her off. "What's to understand? I mean, I've done some crazy stuff—no, tons of crazy stuff—but this is, like, seriously whacked."

Jodi squeezed Kat's arm, and then said, "Hold on a second." She softened her voice a bit. "Listen, Heather. We're not trying to gang up on you here."

"Sure feels like it," Heather said, avoiding eye contact. "Your problem is you're stuck in, like, the Ice Age. Ever heard of a blind date?" She turned to Kat.

"That's way different—," Kat started to say.

Heather waved her off. "Well, it's a new century, if you hadn't noticed, and people meet on the Internet all the time. Plus there's gonna be hundreds of people around that night, right? So I don't see what could possibly go wrong?"

Jodi bit the inside of her lip as she arranged her thoughts. She pressed the point gently. "Um, it *is* kinda unusual. What do your parents think? Are they cool with it?"

"I haven't told them," Heather said. Her eyes darted from Jodi to Kat, and then back to Jodi.

"You mean *yet*—haven't told them *yet*, right?" Jodi asked, and then took another drink from her shake.

"Actually," Heather said, "well, my dad left the country yesterday on some business trip to Paris with my mom. They're gone for, like, ten days, and the prom is this Friday, so it's not like I can just talk to them about it."

Kat cleared her throat.

Jodi almost sprayed her shake. "So you're saying they don't know? You're sure that's a good idea?"

"Don't worry about me," Heather said, yanking open her purse. "I already know what my dad would say." She ripped out a ten-dollar bill and stuffed it by her plate. "And it's not like I'm some fourteen-year-old kid. I can handle things just fine." She stood and headed for the door. Jodi exchanged a look with Kat at the table.

"Hold on, Heather," Jodi said.

Heather stopped and turned around. "What?"

"Let's say he is as wonderful as you say," Jodi said. "Just humor me for a second."

Heather folded her arms.

"Why not spend the night at my house tonight," Jodi said. "I'm sure my parents will say it's fine so you don't have to be home alone. Besides, Kat's already planning to sleep over—"

"Yeah, Jodi's gonna help me learn how to study the Bible and all that stuff," Kat offered.

"We could, like, go on-line together and check out this Mr. Wonderful with you," Jodi said, "just for the fun of it. Deal?" She pulled her hair back into a loose ponytail.

Heather took the car keys out of her pants pocket. "Maybe." With that, she turned and disappeared with a huff.

"What's eating her?" Kat asked.

Jodi had a hunch, but didn't feel right saying anything, at least not yet. After a quick moment, she said, "You know, Kat, I wish I knew."

So what's this called again?" Kat asked. She pulled her legs toward her chest as she sat on the floor of Jodi's bedroom.

"Well, most people call it the Lord's Prayer," Jodi said. She had just finished studying Luke 11:2–4 with Kat, who wanted some advice on how to pray.

"I don't know about that forgiveness stuff," Kat said, shaking her head side to side. "Seems like Jesus is asking a lot of us, don'tcha think?"

Jodi smiled. There was something so very cool about Kat as a young believer, she thought. Jodi loved Kat's honesty. "What's the hardest part for you?"

"Well, it says right here," Kat said, picking up the Bible Jodi bought her. "Um, wait. Oh, here it is: 'Forgive us our sins'—which still blows my mind that he'd do that for me, you know?"

Jodi nodded, and then waited for Kat to finish her thought.

"But then he, um, Jesus says, 'for we also forgive everyone who sins against us.'" Kat stretched her legs out in front of her and laid the Bible down on her lap. "I mean, I'm not sure I can do that, like, all the time—with everybody."

"You can say that again," Jodi said. She twirled several strands of hair around her forefinger. "Sure goes against how I feel most of the time."

Kat played with an earring for a second. "Yeah, but does that mean even if the person doesn't ask to be forgiven for what they've done to you?"

"*Especially* when they haven't asked," Jodi said. "Otherwise we'd be, like, walking around holding all these grudges. Who'd you have in mind?"

"Well, in my case that means my dad." Kat folded her arms. "Gosh, the stuff that man did to me—"

Jodi could see a faraway look cloud Kat's eyes. While Jodi didn't know all the details, she knew Kat's dad was in prison in New Jersey. She reached over and put a hand on Kat's shoulder. She waited a long minute for Kat to speak.

"Um, wow . . . he . . . uh, when I was eleven—" Kat's eyes began to tear up.

"It's okay, it's okay," Jodi said softly. "We don't have to talk about it right now if—"

"No, I'm okay. I . . . I just never told anyone," Kat said. A tear rolled down her cheek. "I remember this guy—a drinking buddy from my dad's work—came to the house when my mom wasn't home."

Jodi reached up for the box of tissues on her dresser and handed it to Kat.

"Thanks." Kat dabbed at her face. "Anyway, he, you know . . . well, I was, like, taking a bath, and this guy barged into the bathroom—" Kat closed her eyes and started to rock back and forth in place.

Jodi put her arm around Kat.

"This jerk said he was there to help me with my bath," Kat managed to say. "I yelled for my dad—boy, did I yell, but he didn't do anything to stop him. And when I told my mom about what happened, you know what she did?"

Jodi shook her head.

"Not a darn thing." Kat drew her legs back up against her chest. "Sure, Mom said something to my dad the next day, but he just laughed it off . . . and that was that—until the next time it happened." Kat looked down. She spoke just above a whisper. "Stuff like this went on until I was almost fourteen."

The two girls sat quietly for several minutes. The only sound came from the fish tank bubbling away next to Jodi's desk. Although Jodi was the Pennsylvania state champ in debate, at the moment she couldn't find the right words to say. How could Kat understand that not every dad was a perv? How could Kat understand the love of a heavenly Father when her earthly father was such a disaster? Jodi prayed a silent prayer for Kat.

"Like two years ago," Kat confided, finally breaking the silence, "I found a whole bunch of porno on my dad's computer. Really sick stuff, you know? By then I was so mad at him, it was kinda easy to call the police. Turns out my dad was selling pictures of underage kids on the Net."

Jodi said, "I'm so very sorry, Kat."

"Yeah, well, he's in jail now, for something like eighteen more years," Kat said. She crossed her arms. "And that's my problem . . . How am I supposed to forgive him? I hate the man . . . Gosh, no wonder I've been so screwed up!" She managed a nervous laugh.

Jodi smiled.

"Maybe that's why I, like, got into the party scene and all," Kat said. "Who knows? Right? The main thing is that I know Jesus loves me now and . . . what was that verse you gave me last weekend?"

Jodi leaned her head to one side. She had typed out several verses on three-by-five cards for Kat. "I think you mean 2 Corinthians 5:17," Jodi said. She recited it from memory: "'Therefore, if anyone is in Christ, he is a new creation; the old has gone, the new has come!'"

"That's the one," Kat said with a smile. She pulled out another tissue and wiped her eyes. "Gosh, sorry to dump all that on you, Jodi."

Jodi started to respond when they heard her mom call down the hall. "Jodi . . . you've got company. Heather's here."

"Be right there, Mom."

"Are you kidding?" Kat said. "My mascara must be a mess."

"You're a nut case!" Jodi teased. She helped Kat stand up. "Come on. Let's rescue Heather from this mystery man."

CHAPTER 3 ✦ WEDNESDAY, 7:33 P.M.

The state prison in Trenton, New Jersey, a gray-stone and red-brick facility, was located on the corner of Second Street and Federal. With no windows and no view, the prison was surrounded by a twenty-foot-high, solid-rock wall, topped with razor-tipped barbed wire. Guard towers outfitted with security cameras and spotlights, situated every fifty feet, overlooked the aging complex.

As if apologizing for its presence in the community, prison officials had ordered that a colorful mural be painted on the neighborhood side of the wall on Second Street several years ago. A touch of graffiti was added by the local street thugs.

A man on a moped maneuvered the low-powered bicycle slowly past the duplexes and row homes that surrounded the prison on three sides. Although the moon hung low in the sky, occasionally obscured behind a cloak of gray clouds, he noticed kids playing stickball under the yellowish haze tossed off by the streetlights.

As he made his way down the street, he saw but didn't acknowledge some of the familiar faces of those who sat drinking beer on the front steps of their homes. The scent of strong, distinctive ethnic cooking filled the night air. He pulled into the parking lot marked "New Jersey Department of Corrections" at the far end of Second Street.

He navigated the speed bumps that littered the parking lot, taking care not to skid on the damp pavement. Typically he avoided driving the moped in foul weather. A light rain had passed through the area several hours prior, delaying his visit until now. He found a spot to park in the shadows, and with a click, snapped the kickstand into place. He liked using the moped since, unlike a car or other vehicle, it didn't require a license plate to operate in the state.

No plate, no way to trace his identity.

He slung his knapsack over his left shoulder and began walking across the lot. He was hampered by a slight limp, thanks to a piece of shrapnel embedded in his leg during a tour of duty in Desert Storm. After pushing his way through the glass front door, he paused briefly. He stood still just inside the visitors' entrance.

Here, the air that greeted his nostrils smelled like a cross between a dirty hamper and Lysol. His glasses, tinted red, which were worn primarily to obscure his features, fogged up from the change in humidity. Rather than remove the frames to wipe the lenses on his shirt, he swiped at them with the back of his gloved hand. Awkward, yes. But to remove the phony lenses would give the guards a clear shot of his face in the security camera.

That done, he presented his knapsack and his New Jersey driver's license at the security desk, knowing full well the license was a forgery. It gave his name as "Elvis Smith," which was a complete fabrication. He was unsure what the penalty would be if he were caught with the bogus credentials. Then again, he wasn't worried. He'd been visiting this penitentiary for several years. So far, no problem.

After all, he was a regular, affording him some frequent-visitor status of sorts. At least that's what he imagined. Half the time the guard didn't bother to compare his face to the doctored photo on the license. He watched as his knapsack was scanned. They wouldn't find any contraband. He wasn't going to take any chances, not now anyway.

An armed guard handed him his bag and then said, "Right this way, Elvis."

He avoided direct eye-to-eye contact as he accepted the knapsack from the guard.

A moment later, Elvis passed through the metal detector and then waited for the faded green-metal door to yield. With a clang, the door slid open on its well-worn track. He stepped into the holding area as the door slammed shut behind him with a convincing clank. Thirty seconds later, the inner door in front of him opened. Another armed guard awaited him inside the belly of the jail.

Elvis was escorted to the visiting area, a room about twenty feet square. No pictures. No carpet. No windows. Just a bare concrete floor and plaster walls painted industrial gray probably a hundred years ago, he guessed. He observed three guards talking in low tones off to one side. He was shown to a seat, a rickety metal folding chair that matched the dull gray walls. He sat facing a two-inch-thick Plexiglas window. He was the only visitor, probably because visiting hours were due to end in about twenty minutes.

Moments later, a man with an unshaven face in an orange jumpsuit appeared at his window.

Elvis picked up the black phone to the left of the partition and pressed the receiver to his ear.

The prisoner did the same, and then spoke first.

"You made me wait—all day. What gives?"

"I'm here, ain't I?" Elvis said, adding, "Cut me some slack."

"Whadya bring me?"

Elvis placed the handset on the stainless-steel ledge beneath the window, reached into his knapsack, and then withdrew a nine-by-twelve unsealed manila envelope. He signaled to the guard, who retrieved it. Elvis watched as the guard reviewed the contents and then delivered it on the other side of the wall.

Elvis picked up the phone and said, "A little cash, something to read, and your cigs, Jake."

Elvis watched as Jake placed a cigarette in his mouth. The guard provided a light. He inhaled deeply. "One of life's simple pleasures," he said. A cloud of smoke gushed out of his nose like a dragon blowing flames.

Jake crossed his legs. "So, tell me. You still using the library?"

"Sure thing," Elvis said. "Mom would be proud. Got us all library cards as kids, you know? Kinda stupid if you ask me. Would've liked a video game—but no, I got a library card instead. Know what I'm saying?"

Jake took another drag, and then balanced the butt of the cigarette on the edge of the window sill. He ignored the question.

"The *same* library?"

"What's it to you?" Elvis snapped.

"I don't like it. You sure they're not on to you?"

Elvis shook his head. "The place is a ghost town—trust me. Everybody's over at Blockbuster. So me, I see the help-desk people napping half the time. We're cool."

Jake picked up the cigarette and held it in front of his lips as he spoke. "Maybe. There's too much at risk—especially now. I say you mix it up a little. See?"

"Whatever," Elvis said with a shrug. "Seems like this place has got you hypersensitive—"

"I'd be real careful if I were you, pal," Jake said slowly. His eyes narrowed. "Serious business. Unless you wanna join me."

"That'll never happen," Elvis said, switching the phone to his left ear.

Jake put the cigarette between his lips and laughed. His was a raspy smoker's cough. "Famous last words. I know a couple of guys in here who'd love to meet you . . . take Dutch. He's 350 pounds of pure steel. You'd be his girlfriend in no time."

"Come on, Jake. I think—"

"That's the problem," Jake said, waving his free hand. "You let me do the thinking for us. See?"

Neither man spoke for a minute.

Elvis was seriously bugged. The way he saw things, he was the one taking all the risks, doing the dirty work. He had more to lose than Jake. If caught, he, not Jake, would spend the rest of his days doing time. The police would never find a trail linking the two men, and Jake, the second he got out, would be off in the Caribbean.

Jake continued. "Listen, when my time's up, I'm countin' on a fat bank account so I can straight-up disappear, you see what I'm saying? You screw up this gig"—he jabbed a finger at the glass window—"I swear, you'll be fish meat."

Elvis knew Jake was dead serious. Five years ago, Jake was double-crossed by a partner, a twenty-something drifter who got too smart for his own good. Although Jake didn't actually provide the cement boots, he paid to have his problem disappear at the bottom of a quarry. If Elvis had any doubts about Jake's threat, one look at the social security number on his bogus driver's license was all the proof he needed. The number was taken from the deceased man.

"Okay—okay," Elvis said. "I'll move things around, big daddy. Keep it cool. Just remember, without me you got nothing."

Jake lit another cigarette with the last ember of his first smoke. "So give me the scoop on things."

"Like I said yesterday, we got fifty thousand subscribers—"

"Tell me something I don't know. We're almost out of time."

"—we're getting hits from Japan, from Denmark . . . Oh, yeah," Elvis said. "There must be a fan club or something in Canada. Big run on the site from Toronto. Go figure."

Jake leaned his head to one side. Holding the cigarette between his thumb and forefinger, he took a drag and leaned forward. "Can the server handle the traffic?"

Elvis nodded. "Not an issue, you know. We got something like 127,000 unique hits last month—lookie loos mostly. Still, no problem with the volume."

Jake scratched his chin. "We've gotta convert more of those first-timers. I say we try the three-tier approach, see what I'm saying?"

"How's that?"

"Give something away free in level one . . . give the regular access on level two for twenty bucks, then," Jake said, "offer a premium package. Maybe pirate video footage or some such jazz. Charge thirty dollars a month."

"Piece of cake." Elvis liked the sound of it. He'd been thinking along the same lines and was about to say so when Jake cut him off.

"Listen, man. You gotta market the heck out of our site." Jake's eyes darted back and forth as he spoke. "Web banners, links, newsgroups, chat rooms . . . who knows how much time we'll get away with this, right?"

Jake looked around the room before he spoke.

"Listen, my man. The beauty is in the simplicity, right? There's no staff. No paper trail. No overhead. Just you and me." He held the cigarette in his mouth.

Elvis smiled. "I know, I know. There's no office for the Feds to bust—"

"We're phantoms," Jake said, uncrossing his legs, the cigarette butt still hanging in his mouth. "And a million bucks a month is just the beginning." He rubbed his hands together.

"You got that right."

"Tell me, Elvis, where's the green?"

"It's, um, offshore. The Cayman Islands. A numbered account. Just like you wanted."

"Untraceable?"

"We're invisible, like air, man. So what's the downside?" Elvis's forehead was crumpled like a wad of paper.

"How long do you plan to be dumb?" Jake said. "Don't make me spell it out—"

"The, uh, remains—"

"Exactly." Jake shot Elvis a look. "You've got to be so dang careful, you hear? Still using the scrapmetal yard?"

Elvis nodded.

"Maybe try the quarry."

"Okay, I'm good with that." Elvis hated the thought of using the quarry, but didn't have time to argue the point. "Listen, bro, I've got some stuff I need to do. I'll be seeing you." Elvis hung up the receiver and turned to leave.

Jake whacked on the glass with his handset.

Elvis spun back around, picked up the phone and listened.

"You keep your nose clean, see? No slip-ups, either," Jake said. "I hear otherwise, I'll give the word and you'll be swimming for a very long time."

Elvis turned and then left the building.

Billy Bender shed the thick glasses the moment he left the prison grounds. When he was three miles from the prison, he pulled his moped into the Kmart parking lot. He parked next to a thirty-foot recreation vehicle and unlocked the storage bin behind the rear tires.

With a grunt, he stashed his moped inside, and then glanced around as he closed the compartment. Satisfied that he hadn't been followed, he climbed behind the wheel of the two-year-old RV, fired up the engine, and then disappeared into traffic on the main road.

You guys think I'm clueless," Heather complained, crossing her arms. She sat on the beige leather sofa in the family room, her legs tucked back to one side. Jodi and Kat occupied the matching sofa across from her. They'd been arguing ever since Heather arrived at Jodi's house, and Jodi was ready to pull her hair out.

"Listen, Heather," Jodi said, lifting her feet off the coffee table. "You're, like, blowing things way out of proportion over nothing. Why is it that when Kat and I express our, um—"

"—concern," Kat offered.

"Right, our *concern* about this guy," Jodi repeated, "you get all defensive? Like I said a hundred times, he may actually be a great guy—I'll give you that." She picked at the ends of her hair. "Still, I don't know, he could be a psycho too. We just want to make sure."

Heather turned her head to the side for a second. "Just so you know, I'm not some ditzy blonde. And I'm not some sheltered kid without a clue—"

"Nobody thinks that," Kat said. "But come on, Heather. You said it yourself . . . you've never even met the guy, and you're going to go with him to the prom? *Please.* How smart is that?"

Jodi rolled up the sleeves of her sweatshirt. "Plus, there've been stories all over the news about girls getting raped by these creeps at the mall or wherever."

"Yeah, I saw something on, like, *Dateline* when I was in the hospital last weekend," Kat said. "Some girl met this guy on-line, and she, um, she agreed to get together with him at a hotel—no . . . at the mall, that's it. He shows up with, like, duct tape and a knife. Not good. He beat and raped her and she almost died."

"John's different," Heather argued. "I just know it—"

"How can you be so sure?" Kat said, cutting her off. "What if he's a ninety-five-year-old rapist?"

"At least I could outrun him." Heather smiled, her first of the evening. "Besides, I've got John's picture and he's no grandpa."

"This guy, John," Jodi said, "he sent the picture *to* you, right?"

"Yeah," Heather said. "And I'd say he looks seventeen, maybe eighteen."

Kat laughed. "Come on, girl. He's probably a rapist who sends everybody the same picture of some hottie he cut out of, like, a muscle magazine just to draw them in."

"Exactly what I was thinking." Jodi looked at Kat with a nod.

Heather shook her head. "You're both way wrong and I can prove it."

"Good. Do it. Right now," Kat said. She hooked her hair behind her left ear.

"Fine. Take me to your computer," Heather said, looking in the direction of the desk in the corner of the room.

"All right." Jodi stood and stretched. "This should be interesting."

Heather and Kat followed Jodi to the desk. The computer was in sleep mode. With a click of the space bar the computer sprang back to life. Jodi double-clicked on the America Online icon and then pulled out the swivel chair. She said, "It's all yours."

Heather sat down and logged on using the guest feature.

"This I gotta see," Kat said, pulling up a chair next to Heather. Jodi leaned against the wall and peered over their shoulders.

"Okay, here we go," Heather said. She typed in her AOL screen name, IluvHim4Ever2, and her password. "Hold on a second. I've gotta change my preferences so my buddy list knows I'm on-line."

A moment later, the AOL system announced: "You've got mail." Heather clicked on the mail icon and scanned the seven incoming e-mail items. "See," she said, pointing to one. "It's from John." She pointed to the e-mail from JesusFreakster2.

"JesusFreakster2?" Kat said. "Sounds bogus to me."

"Knock it off, Kat." Jodi swatted Kat across the back.

"All right, watch this." Heather clicked on her list of favorite places. "I checked out John's personal Web page—without him knowing it." The page took several seconds to load.

"Yeah," Kat countered, "I bet he wanted you to check it out so you'd think he was real."

"Actually, you're wrong, Kat" Heather said, turning to Kat as she spoke. "He never told me he *had* a Web page. I just snooped around. I went to his, like, AOL profile and found his link to this page. Plus, I verified that he goes to Villanova High School through their yearbook."

"Oh, there's Mr. Wonderful," Kat said after the page loaded. "He *is* hot. Nice tan, too. Probably got it in a bottle—"

This time Jodi and Heather gave Kat a swat, although Jodi had to agree that the dark-haired guy on the screen did have awesome abs. He looked really good in faded blue jeans, and, she thought, his soft brown eyes dripped with warmth. *No wonder Heather is melting*, Jodi thought.

"Okay, let's see," Jodi began, squinting at the screen. "Under favorite music . . . says he's been to a dc Talk concert . . . likes P.O.D. . . . the Newsboys . . . and thinks some pop music is cool, too."

"Yeah, and as if his hobby is really horseback riding," Kat said, pointing to a spot on the screen. "The only horse he's ever been on was probably on a merry-go-round as a kid."

"You don't have to be so mean," Heather said. "You're just jealous, that's all."

"Says he's into snowboarding, skateboarding, and basketball, too," Kat said. "A regular jock. I say, fat chance."

Jodi pointed to another place on the page. "Shh, Kat. Look, there's his favorite Scripture verse: John 3:16."

"See," Heather said, glancing over her shoulder at Jodi. "He's a Christian, just like I told you."

On the surface it appeared that Heather had done her homework, Jodi thought. Maybe Heather really had met a cool Christian guy. Yet something bothered her. But what? What was missing? *Nothing.* That's it, she decided. Everything fit a little too nicely.

"Heather," Jodi said. "Um, you said you saw John in the yearbook, right?"

Heather nodded. "Yeah. I just followed the link from his Web page to the school's yearbook."

"I'm just curious. What did he look like?"

"What do you mean?" Heather turned halfway around.

"His picture," Jodi said. "In the yearbook. What did he look like?"

Jodi saw hesitation in Heather's eyes.

"Well, I didn't exactly see his picture there," Heather admitted, biting her lip. "But his name was listed right there with the other seniors."

Jodi raised her right eyebrow but didn't say anything.

"Gosh, so the guy missed picture day. What's the big deal?" Heather turned back to the monitor.

Jodi cleared her throat. "Doesn't that strike you as a little bit *convenient?*"

"Convenient?"

Jodi placed a hand on Heather's shoulder. "Yeah, I mean . . . well, just think about it. This guy, like, claims to be John Knox, who goes to Villanova High. But you have no way of knowing whether this picture," she said, pointing to the screen, "is really the same kid as the John Knox who goes to school, now do you?"

Before Heather could answer, a musical tone played through the computer speakers announcing the arrival of a knock-knock.

"It's John," Heather said. "Oh my gosh, what should I do?"

The girls immediately hovered around the monitor and studied the instant-message screen that had popped up.

Jodi felt her heart leap. "Answer him!"

Kat elbowed Heather. "Whatcha waiting for?"

"All right already," Heather said, clicking the ACCEPT button to receive the message.

JesusFreakster2:	wuz up? U busy?
IluvHim4Ever2:	nm U?
JesusFreakster2:	can't wait til Friday
IluvHim4Ever2:	me2!!!
JesusFreakster2:	by the way I, rented a limo

Kat whistled through her teeth. "This guy's like really in the dough. Must be nice."

"Shh," Heather said.

"Duh. As if he can hear us," Kat said with a laugh.

IluvHim4Ever2:	WOW I lv limos
JesusFreakster2:	Is 5:30 good?
IluvHim4Ever2:	Sounds great!
JesusFreakster2:	Don't worry, there's no hot tub on this 1
IluvHim4Ever2:	lol

"Tell him you want to meet—tomorrow," Jodi blurted out.

Heather turned and stared at her. "What?"

Jodi nodded toward the keyboard. "You want to prove he's for real. So go on—do it. Kat and I will be there just in case."

"I—I don't know . . . You think so? Where?" Heather asked.

Jodi considered this for a quick second. "Meet him at Johnny Angel's."

Heather faced the computer and tapped the keyboard with her forefinger for several seconds, a nervous habit. She tilted her head to one side and then typed the message.

IluvHim4Ever2:	what ru doing tomorrow?
JesusFreakster2:	I dunno
IluvHim4Ever2:	I think we should meet, like at 4
JesusFreakster2:	y?
IluvHim4Ever2:	I dunno. Just 2 talk. B nice to cu
JesusFreakster2:	k, where?

"Oh my gosh," Kat squealed, almost jumping out of her chair. "The little weasel is gonna do it—"

"KAT!" said Jodi and Heather in unison.

"What? What did I say?"

"Would you shush?" Jodi said to Kat. She leaned toward Heather's ear. "Okay, now don't tell him we're gonna be there."

IluvHim4Ever2:	Johnny Angel's near my school
JesusFreakster2:	cool. 4 it is
IluvHim4Ever2:	hey I g2g
JesusFreakster2:	c-ya then
IluvHim4Ever2:	bye!!
JesusFreakster2:	adios chica, hehe

"There. Are you guys all happy now?" Heather said. She flipped her hair over her left shoulder in the direction of Kat. "You'll see what a great guy he is."

"Uh-huh," Kat said skeptically. "Aren't you nervous?"

"Are you kidding?" Heather said. "My heart is only pounding so hard it's gonna burst!"

"Wait a second," Jodi said as Heather was about to sign off. "Aren't you gonna check his e-mail?"

"Right. With you two vultures looking over my shoulder?" Heather quipped.

"I won't look—promise!" Kat said.

"Me neither," Jodi said, tugging at Kat's arm. "Come on. We'll go grab some ice cream while you read his note."

"Okay, I'll be just a sec," Heather said.

Jodi, who was halfway to the kitchen, turned around. "Yeah, and stop drooling on my computer!"

CHAPTER 5 ✳ THURSDAY, 7:15 A.M.

The Kamp of the Woods RV park was an upscale facility nestled along the New Jersey side of the Delaware River just across from Philadelphia. Its thirty acres of heavily wooded, mature trees made it a popular spot for vacationers, as the location afforded privacy and yet proximity to historic city sites. With the beach destinations as close as a snappy forty-five-minute drive down the Atlantic City Expressway, Kamp of the Woods's 110 spots stayed packed almost year-round.

Ronnie and Gloria Mason were frequent guests of the park. They enjoyed the in-ground pool, full hookups, phone access at each site, pit grill, tennis courts, and the familiar faces of other retirees who vacationed there. Because it offered an easy walk to the main office, gift shop, and coin-operated laundry, they had been renting the same spot, space 22, for ten years.

Although Ronnie had retired five years ago, he and Gloria were still healthy, active, and just pushing seventy. Retirement was getting boring, and Ronnie, with his pioneer spirit, was in the market for something to occupy his time besides reading books and fishing. When they learned the owners of the Kamp of the Woods wanted to sell, they jumped at the opportunity to explore buying the campground.

Thanks to a lifetime of good fiscal planning, Ronnie and Gloria had enough in the way of investments to secure the down payment on the property. Their good credit, coupled with the camp's solid track record of profitability, made securing a business loan a breeze. They had spent the last three weeks working through the mountains of paperwork necessary to seal the deal. Now all they had left to do was wait for the bank to finalize their documents.

The aroma of fresh coffee filled the RV as Gloria carried the pot to the table. She took a seat at the modest, foldout table across from Ronnie, who remained immersed in the newspaper. She poured his mug two-thirds full, and having forgotten the creamer, set the pot on a colorful handmade potholder. She made her way to the refrigerator, retrieved a pint of half-and-half, and was about to return to the table when she saw someone working on the RV adjacent to theirs.

"Oh, look, honey," Gloria said. "It's that nice boy—"

"Huh?" Ronnie turned a page of the paper.

"The one who's been next door ever since we got here."

"I guess," he said.

She parted a space in the miniblinds for a better view. "Gee, I wonder what such a nice young fellow is doing all alone on the road."

Ronnie coughed.

She looked over at her husband. "I can't say that I've seen anybody with him. Don't you think that's odd?"

"Uh-huh. You got that creamer?"

She stole another look out the window. "Coming right up." She walked to the table and placed the creamer next to his cup, distracted. "Seems he's always coming and going at all hours. You know, I think he must have some sort of an eye condition."

"Uh, how's that?"

"Well, it's just that he always wears those red-tinted glasses."

Ronnie put down his newspaper and fixed his coffee.

"He works with computers, you know," Gloria said.

"Is that so?"

Gloria nodded, smoothing out her skirt. "Yes, it is. He and I bumped into each other at the front office. Actually, he was paying his bill, and I was there picking out a postcard. His name is Elvis something. I remembered the Elvis part since it's such an unusual name and all. Anyway, he and I left the building at the same time, so we talked on the way back here. Nice guy."

Ronnie picked up his paper again.

"Honey, you know how we've been having problems with that new laptop?" she asked, and then waited for a response. When none came, she added, "Are you listening to me, dear?"

"Yes, sweetie." He discarded several pages and then focused on the sports section.

"Well," she continued, pouring herself a cup, "you know how the kids got us that computer so we can stay in touch?"

"Yes, dear."

"Only we haven't been able to get the confounded thing to work right. I think I'll ask him if he can help us."

"You do that," Ronnie said. "You're the social butterfly in the family."

"Well, he did offer, you know." She sipped her coffee.

"Who did?"

"Elvis."

Ronnie managed a laugh. He looked at her over the top of his reading glasses. "You want Elvis to fix our computer? I thought Elvis was dead."

She reached across the table and squeezed his hand. "No, silly goose, not that Elvis. I knew you weren't listening."

Ronnie smiled. "I'm just kidding, sweetie. I think it's a great idea."

"If I didn't know you better, I'd say you were lying through your teeth," Gloria said with a wink. "Anyway, like I always say, no time like the present." With that, Gloria rose, opened the door and stepped outside.

"You-hoo, Mr. Elvis . . . good morning," she said, waving her hand as she crossed the twenty feet between them.

Elvis looked up, startled. "Hi, Mrs. . . . "

"Mason. Gloria Mason," she prompted. "Remember, we met in the office?"

"Um, that's right," Elvis said, glancing around. "What's up? How's the mister?"

"Oh, Ronnie? He's just fine," she said with a look at their RV. "I've been meaning to ask you something."

His eyes shifted back and forth. "Shoot."

"Well," Gloria began, flattening her skirt, "I'm sorry to disturb you. But we were wondering if you could help us figure out how to get on-line with that computer we have. Seems we're from the old school. Our kids bought it for us so we could keep in touch, you know."

"Uh, sure thing," he said. A loose piece of gravel, with a ping, leaped three inches when he shifted the toe of his boot. "I'm just about done fixing my satellite connection. When's good with you?"

"Actually, I've just made a fresh pot of coffee, if you've got a minute now," she said, a pleasant smile plastered on her face. "I always say, no time like the present." Gloria studied him as he checked his watch.

"Um, sure . . . I've got a couple of minutes now. Let's see what you got," he said. His eyes narrowed as they darted from her to her RV.

For a split second, Gloria felt a degree of uneasiness, although she couldn't pinpoint why—perhaps it was the odd way he licked his lips. But she quickly dismissed the thought.

Back inside his RV, the shades drawn tight, Billy stared at a spot on the wall.

Of all the bad luck, he had to be parked next to a nosy neighbor. Under most circumstances, he liked to park in a slot toward the rear of an RV park where he and his activities were removed from meddlesome campers. Everything counted on anonymity. But not this time. The park was at full capacity. He was fortunate to have a slot at all, and he knew it.

On the other hand, the morning wasn't a complete waste.

While configuring their laptop and testing their access to the Internet, he used the occasion to upload some of his files to his Web site. And, although he pretended to look the other way while Gloria typed in her password, he couldn't help but see—given that she typed with one finger—it was "Trixie." That wasn't a real surprise either, considering she bent his ear about their now-deceased dog the whole time he was working.

But something else bothered him.

He wasn't sure Gloria had bought his excuse for working with black leather gloves. Naturally, there was no way he'd leave his fingerprints on their system. He explained the gloves were designed to prevent carpal tunnel, a numbing of the hands. He claimed they were essential for people like himself who worked on a keyboard all day.

This morning changed everything. Just to be sure he couldn't be fingered by them, he'd have to leave the campground. But not yet, he decided. He had way too much to do in the next twenty-four hours, and he couldn't be bothered with the hassle of relocating again.

Billy blinked. He stood, turned around, and then lifted the cushion on the bench seat where he had been sitting. He opened the space-saving compartment hidden from view by the cushion. He withdrew a dark green duffel bag and then placed it on the carpet.

He crouched down, unzipped the bag, and examined its contents: two rolls of duct tape, a seven-inch knife, and a 9mm Australian-made Glock with the serial numbers filed off. He picked up the gun and checked the action.

The weapon was his favorite, something he'd purchased at a flea market. Although it wasn't his only handgun, he loved the weight and balance of the piece. He returned the Glock to the bag, laying it next to a silencer and three ammo clips. Each double-stack magazine held ten bullets. They were full.

He briefly thumbed through ten stacks of hundred-dollar bills. Each stack contained one hundred, bound together. The total stash was worth $100,000. Pocket change to him. Plenty more where that came from.

He quickly verified the condition of the four remote-controlled, lipstick-sized cameras, a miniaturized digital video recorder no larger than a Palm Pilot, a length of four-strand rope, and a shiny brass nametag.

"Okay, it's almost showtime," he said under his breath.

He zipped the bag shut.

Hey man, you want lunch?"

Agent Nick Steele looked up from his bank of computers. Dwayne Whitmore, his new partner, stood in the doorway. A thirty-seven-year-old FBI agent, Dwayne had recently been assigned to Nick in the Philadelphia Field Office, and, Nick figured, he was attempting to make a good first impression.

At sixty-two, Nick, a thirty-year veteran of the FBI, was in charge of the Bureau's anti-cyberporn program, dubbed "Innocent Images." He pushed back from his desk and laughed. "You kidding? I'm still recovering from that soul food you brought me yesterday." Nick reached for his half-filled Styrofoam cup of coffee. "This is about all I can handle."

"That's cool," Dwayne said. "Thought I'd ask. You need anything, just give a shout." He lingered in the doorway.

Nick pointed over his shoulder at the computer screen. "What I need is to catch this creep."

"I heard that," Dwayne said with a nod. "What's up?"

"This guy is one heck of a snake," Nick said, scratching the side of his face. "He's smart. He knows all the right words. And he's had plenty of practice. You got a second to take a look?"

"Sure thing." Dwayne walked over to Nick's desk, pushed several files aside and then sat on the edge, keeping one foot on the floor. "You got a name for him?"

"Still working on that." Nick leaned back in his swivel chair. "Okay. We do know he's not your typical traveler," he said. "Most cyber-predators are bored, middle-aged men looking to cheat on their wives— or maybe they're loners with no social skills, right?"

"Yeah," Dwayne agreed, crossing his arms. "Those dudes get their kicks preying on kids—"

"Usually impressionable young girls, at that," Nick added. "Most work 'em several weeks, maybe months. They're patient. Whatever it takes to create an emotional bond with these misunderstood girls. For what?" Nick took a sip from his cup before answering his own question. "For the sex. But not this guy. He's not into the sex. He's working a different racket."

"So lay it on me," Dwayne said. "What's his gig?"

"His approach is about the same as most travelers. He meets his victims—usually girls, sometimes boys—by lurking in a chat room," Nick said. "He flatters 'em, tells 'em how wonderful they are. He plays 'em like a violin. They pour out their little hearts . . . give him personal info, pictures, even their home address. Why? 'Cause suddenly, he's their best friend—even though he avoids giving them any real info in exchange."

"Let me guess," Dwayne said, massaging his temples. "The perp grooms several peeps at the same time. Am I right?"

Nick nodded. "But this guy somehow vaporizes his trail."

"You know how he's doing it?"

"I'd say he's using an anonymous remailer to scrub out his back-tracking info." Nick tossed his empty cup into the trash. "It clears out his personal data, making a cybertrace next to impossible. And he likes to IM the kids. IM's don't leave any footprints in cyberspace—not unless someone uses special computer software to capture the dialogue."

Dwayne let out a whistle. "And a kid being scammed ain't about to do that."

"Exactly. I know these perverts like the back of my bald head—heck, I could write a book on 'em," Nick said. "But this time, it's different. Here." He beckoned with his hand. "I want you to see something, if you've got the stomach for it."

"You're the boss," Dwayne said. "Lunch'll wait." He pulled up a folding chair.

Nick hammered away at his keyboard. "Take a look."

Dwayne watched as the Web site MegaFear.com loaded. "What's with this?"

"He's selling fear."

"Say what?" Dwayne leaned toward the screen.

"Fear," Nick said. "Ever watch one of those 'reality' TV shows . . . the ones where they scare the heck out of some unsuspecting soul?"

"No, boss, can't say I have."

Nick reached his hand around the base of Dwayne's thick neck. "Welcome to cheap thrills for bored and numbed couch potatoes of America."

"I heard that, but ain't it illegal?"

Nick shrugged. "Not the stuff on TV. See, they get a signed release— after the fact. People will do anything for their fifteen minutes of fame." Nick cleared his throat. "But this situation appears to be different. As best I can tell, our perp has hijacked a Web-based server, set up a lucra- tive subscription-based service, and provides sickos with gruesome clips of raw, actual fear captured in video clips—my guess is without obtain- ing their permission."

Dwayne looked at Nick. "What's the traveler connection?"

"That's what I'm trying to figure out," Nick said. He folded his arms. "I think we've got a guy who arranges a meeting with the kids he's be- friended in these chat rooms, abducts them, and then subjects them to various fright stimuli—"

"Such as—"

"You name it, this degenerate does it. Watch this." Nick typed in sev- eral commands that bypassed the MegaFear.com sign-in screen. With his mouse he pointed and then clicked on an icon marked "Faces of Fear."

The men both focused on the screen as the video clip loaded. Nick continued. "He brutalizes his victims with rats, dogs, firebrands—and, get this, he videotapes their screams, their panic, their attempts to escape. Some break arms, legs, or bleed—"

The video clip began to play. Bloodcurdling screams filled the speak- ers as a girl tried to distance herself from a ravenous Doberman pinscher who was released into a twenty-by-twenty-foot cage.

Dwayne's eyes widened. After several seconds, he said, "I've seen enough. So . . . then what? Hasn't anybody fingered the dude? You know, after the fact."

Nick closed the screen. "That's the strangest part."

Dwayne slid his chair back a few feet. "Yeah?"

"We got zip," Nick said with a snap his fingers. "Normally, a victim would come forward with a bizarre tale of torture or abduction, and we'd have something to work with."

"Meaning . . ."

"Meaning either the kids aren't talking 'cause they're afraid of what might happen—by the perp, or by their parents," Nick said. "Or . . . maybe they aren't around to talk."

"Which means they're pushing up daisies."

Nick leaned his head to one side. "Could be. I've got a contact on the Philly police force with a witness who reports seeing late-night activity at the scrapmetal plant down by the airport."

Neither man spoke. Nick fiddled with his FBI ID credentials, a picture ID card encased in plastic, hanging on a beaded metal chain around his neck.

"Man, that's twisted," Dwayne said after a long moment. "So why doesn't the Bureau shut him down?"

Nick laughed. "How many agents do we have?"

"Nationwide? Something like ten thousand . . . plus or minus."

"And how many are working with the Homeland Security or anti-terrorist effort?"

"Just about everybody—"

"Exactly." Nick cracked his knuckles. "And how many people use the Internet?"

"Only millions," Dwayne said with a laugh.

"That's why we can't afford to make a mistake here. So we wait."

"Wait for what?"

"We build an airtight case," Nick said, tossing a file toward Dwayne. "That's everything I've got so far. Read it. I need your help to identify this jerk."

"What about my other—"

Nick raised a finger to his lips. "You're the best computer hack on my team. I need you on this, like, yesterday." Nick stood and then walked Dwayne to the door. "I'll reassign your stack to one of the other agents."

"Thanks, man. We'll nail him," Dwayne said. "Our guy will make a mistake—they always do." He tapped the file against the side of his leg. "So tell me, how'd you get this much on him?"

Nick smiled. "Every agent has his trade secrets, I guess."

"That so, sir?" Dwayne said. "Me? I'd probably just ask my fifteen-year-old boy—he's even a better hacker than me." He laughed as he turned to leave.

"Oh, and Dwayne?"

He spun around.

"Better skip lunch."

"How's that?"

"I picked up a transmission to the MegaFear Web site and was able to trace it back to a computer somewhere in Cherry Hill, New Jersey," Nick said.

"When?"

"A couple of hours ago—around eight," Nick said. "I think our man is about to strike again. Get busy."

CHAPTER 7 ✦ THURSDAY, 3:47 P.M.

In an attempt not to be too obvious, Jodi, Kat, and Heather arrived at Johnny Angel's in separate cars. Once inside, Jodi and Kat sat facing each other in a booth against the wall opposite the TO GO counter. Although the plates and trash from the last occupants had yet to be cleared away, Jodi had a perfect view of the front door. Two tables to her right, Heather sat by herself at a four-top in the center of the room, also facing the door.

Kat glanced at Heather for the fifth time in two minutes, and Jodi was about to wring her neck. "Stop staring," Jodi said, her voice low. "You're making her nervous."

Kat laughed. "I'm making her nervous?" She pointed toward her chest with her right hand. "Hardly. You saw the way Heather was at school. She's already a bundle of nerves."

"Well, who wouldn't be?" Jodi couldn't believe Heather was determined to go to the prom with the mystery guy. It was almost as if Heather was trying to prove something, Jodi thought. All day she had been praying that Heather wouldn't let her feelings cloud her judgment. If the guy was a creep—or worse, a smooth operator—Jodi prayed Heather would see the truth and drop him.

Kat fiddled with the in-booth jukebox selector mounted on the wall between them. "I think she's actually, like, glad we're doing this, don't you?"

Jodi nodded. "You know what my dad said?"

"You told him about this?"

"Kat, you said it yourself . . . the guy could be a rapist or something," Jodi said. "I thought he ought to know what we're doing—"

"You're such a straight arrow," Kat stated evenly. She played with an earring. "I mean—don't get me wrong—I really like that about you. Maybe one day I'll be—" Her voice trailed off as she looked toward the door. "So anyway, what'd he say?"

Jodi raked her hand through her hair. "He said he was proud of me— of us—for standing by our friend."

"He said that?" Kat's eyes widened. "Wow. Your dad's cool."

Jodi smiled. "And he reminded me of a verse in Proverbs." She thought for a second, and then recited, "'There is a friend that sticks closer than a brother.'"

Kat appeared puzzled. "I don't get it."

"I think it means that not all friends are alike, you know?" Jodi started to pile the dirty plates by the edge of the table. "Some will, like, stab you in the back. Others hang with you no matter what."

"I heard that," Kat said with a nod, and then stole another look at Heather.

"Listen, Kat," Jodi said. "Now that you're a Christian, stuff like choosing good friends is really important. Take Heather." This time Jodi looked in Heather's direction. "I'd do anything for her. She'd do the same for me, I just know she would." Jodi repositioned herself in the booth so that her legs stretched across the seat. "Sure, sometimes I want to scratch out her eyes—"

Kat laughed.

"—but we really try to, like, encourage each other in our faith, you know?"

Kat checked her watch. "What's with Bruce? He's late. It's almost four."

"Chill. He'll be here," Jodi said. "He's probably kissing that car of his."

They both laughed.

Actually, Jodi admired the way Bruce had been restoring his vintage Mustang. But she knew that sometimes he got so wrapped up in working on it, he lost track of time.

"Hey, got a quarter?" Kat asked.

"Sure, why?"

"You'll see in a sec." The right edge of Kat's lip curled into a mischievous smile.

Jodi fished the coin from her purse. She slid it across the table.

Kat punched her selection, "B-3," into the jukebox. Seconds later, Elvis filled the restaurant with "Heartbreak Hotel."

"That's so bad," Jodi said, tossing a dirty napkin at her.

"Gross!" She tossed it back as if it were laced with anthrax.

"Listen, Kat. You want to know what I think this is all about?"

"With Elvis Presley?"

Jodi shook her head. "No, retard," she said laughing, and then lowered her voice. "With Heather and this guy."

"Tell me."

Jodi bit her lip. "You might not know this but, um, Heather never heard her dad say 'I love you.'"

"Yeah, I heard her say something like that over spring break," Kat said, leaning forward. "I sure know the feeling—and it sucks."

Jodi's thoughts drifted to her conversation with Kat the night before. She looked down at the tile floor and then back to Kat. "What you might not know is why her dad, like, shuts her out." Jodi's eyes met Kat's. "See, when Heather was born, her biological mother died giving birth to her. Heather's dad and mom were high-school sweethearts. Even though he remarried, I think he never forgave Heather—"

"As if she did it on purpose," Kat said.

"My point exactly." Jodi stole a look at Heather. "So, like, I think when she hears this guy all gushing over her, she—"

"—gets taken in," Kat finished the thought, nodding. "Might be. All I know is, this is some crazy stunt."

Out of the corner of her eye, Jodi saw the door open. "Don't look now, but Bruce just walked in."

Kat checked her watch. "It's twelve after four. So where's Mr. Wonderful?"

"Right here," Bruce said, sporting a cheesy grin. He appeared at the table in a Phillies T-shirt and loose jeans.

Jodi shook her head. "Sit down before we deck you, man." She moved her legs to the floor, making room for him.

"Thanks." He plopped down beside Jodi. "Looks like you guys ate without me."

"Actually, we're still waiting for somebody to clear the table," Kat said.

"Sorry I'm late," Bruce apologized. "I was putting a new speaker system in my car. You should hear it—it's killer. So, what did I miss?"

"I told you he was kissing his car," Jodi said, nudging him.

Kat laughed.

Bruce looked sideways at Jodi. "What?"

Jodi waved him off. "Hey, wasn't Stan going to ride with you?" She had suggested that both Bruce and Stan hang out with them in case Heather's Internet buddy turned out to be a creep.

"Actually, he bailed . . . said something came up. So tell me. Any sign of the ax murderer?"

"Shh," Jodi said. "Not so loud—"

"Whoa, I forgot I'm sitting next to the volume police!"

Jodi watched as the waitress approached the table with a gray tub. The woman quickly tossed the plates and trash inside. "You ready to order?" She wiped the table with a rag that smelled to Jodi as if it had been washed sometime during the last century.

"Um, any chance we could snag a few menus?" Bruce asked.

"Sure thing, hon." She pulled three menus from her apron and then disappeared with the tub.

"That might be the last we see of her today," Kat said.

"Let's hope not," Bruce said, scanning the menu options. "I'm thinking a cheese steak, fried onions with extra sauce, um, and fries and a Coke will do me." He patted his stomach. Jodi wondered how guys could pack away so much food.

"How can you eat all that at a time like this?" Kat asked.

"Yeah, I might manage a shake," Jodi said. She glanced at the clock on the wall. Twenty minutes after four. The guy was a no-show, she thought. Jodi leaned forward to look past Bruce at Heather. As their eyes met, Jodi couldn't miss the sad expression on Heather's face. With a wave of her hand, Jodi urged Heather to join them.

Heather grabbed her purse, walked over to the booth, and then plopped down, blowing her bangs as she sat. "What a waste of time— sorry, guys."

The waitress reappeared and looked at Heather. "You decided to join the others. So whatcha want?"

Heather hooked her hair over her left ear. "How about a handsome guy, six-foot-two, dark hair, tanned—"

"Don't we all wish for that, dear," the waitress said, chewing a mouthful of gum.

Bruce coughed.

"Well, maybe not you, son," she added. "So, anybody ready to order?"

Jodi held up her forefinger. "Excuse me, ma'am. I was just wondering something . . . Do you know if a guy happened to come in here looking for somebody, maybe earlier?"

"Jodi!" Heather blurted out, her eyes as wide as saucers.

"Heather, chill. You never know—"

The waitress put a hand on her hip. "You wouldn't happen to be Heather Barnes?"

Jodi thought Heather's face turned pale.

"Uh, ya, I am. Why?" Heather tossed Jodi a look.

"Seems you must have a secret admirer. Give me a second." With that, the waitress circled back to the kitchen.

Kat said, "Wow, Heather. You look like you've seen a ghost."

"Yeah, Heather, breathe," Bruce said. "You know, come up for air— or I'll just have to give you CPR."

Everybody laughed. Jodi knew Bruce hoped to one day become a paramedic. But his dopey grin was more than she could handle. A moment later the waitress returned carrying flowers and a card.

"Here you go, hon."

Heather took the items. "Oh my gosh, wow!"

"Gosh, a dozen roses," Kat said. "I told you he was rich. Come on, open the card . . . Here, I'll hold those for you."

Jodi watched as Heather opened and then read the card to herself.

"What's the deal?" Bruce asked, reaching for the note.

Heather pulled it back, her face flushed. "Okay, it's from John. Here's what he said. Ready?" She flipped her hair over her left shoulder. "John says how sorry and disappointed he was that he couldn't meet me. His younger brother fell and broke his arm on the playground at school. And he had to take him to get a cast put on. He can't wait to see me tomorrow. That's about it." She started to put the card in her purse.

"Whoa! Time out," Bruce said. "You skipped the juicy parts. Come on, Heather, let's have it all—"

"Yeah, and so much for the ax-murderer angle," Kat said.

While Kat and Bruce tried to pry the details out of Heather, Jodi bit her bottom lip. She was bothered that John's last-minute emergency seemed, again, a little too convenient. *Why couldn't his mom or dad take the kid brother?* Jodi thought. *And if this was such an unexpected emergency, when did he have time to buy flowers and get a card?* As she saw it, the flowers only served to mask the fact that John didn't show his face.

Jodi picked through her hair, spying out split ends. *Boy, is this guy slick,* she thought. *Why can't Heather see it?*

CHAPTER 8 ✦ THURSDAY, 7:50 P.M.

The awareness of imminent danger, like a sixth sense, grew with every mile as Billy approached the entrance to the Kamp of the Woods campground. He checked his rearview mirror, swallowing hard but seeing nothing unusual. A minute later, he slowed to pull off the main road into the entrance. His heart, as if it had a mind of its own, started to race.

His eyes darted across the horizon for signs of any unusual activity. The sun had already set, and the moon was taking its time to appear. Fortunately, the check-in area was well lit. There he spied a late-model brown Ford Taurus parked by the front office. He squinted. The government plates sent the hair on the back of his neck skyward as the probability sank in.

He'd been found out.

But how? His mind zipped through the possible explanations. He never used his computer to transmit data. Then again, he'd uploaded some data from Gloria's computer that morning. Was that it? He was confident he'd left no physical fingerprints, thanks to the gloves. And he'd been careful to purge his electronic trail. Still, they'd managed to trace him.

He shook his head in disbelief.

On the other hand there could be any number of reasons why the brown sedan was here. He considered that for a moment. They could be the IRS—not the FBI—doing a spot audit. Maybe the owners were engaged in laundering money. Could be the government on the trail of a missing person, he thought.

He had to be sure. If the FBI was here for him, they held his ticket to prison, maybe even death row.

Billy bristled as he maneuvered his black Nissan Frontier pickup truck, which he had fitted with a Leer camper top, past the office. He turned left down the gravel stretch of driveway where his RV was parked, driving slow enough to survey the surroundings—but not too slow. Even though his windows were tinted black, Billy slid down in the leather seat. No point drawing unnecessary attention to himself.

When the nose of his truck was almost parallel with campsite 22, the space assigned to Gloria, he glanced to the right and noticed two additional government cars. The FBI—of that he now felt certain. In the near blackness, he observed men in dark suits, agents to be sure, covering the front and back of Gloria's motor home. He figured several more must be inside, guns drawn, reading Gloria and her husband the riot act.

Billy gripped the steering wheel, his throat suddenly dry. What had Gloria told them? What could she tell them? How much did she know? Nothing, really. He silently hoped she might forget to mention his help that morning. He was, after all, just setting up her e-mail account. There was nothing suspicious about that. Odds were that was a pipe dream. More likely, the FBI spent several hours tearing apart her computer once they learned "Elvis" from next door had worked on it.

Yet, it was a very real possibility that the Feds had just arrived and hadn't learned anything—so far.

There was no way he could know.

It was just as likely that the agents were sitting with her drinking coffee, waiting for him to come home so she could ID him. He didn't believe in coincidences, and he assumed the worst. The FBI must have enough to hang him—or at least to bring him in for questioning.

Billy knew this day might come, and he wasn't about to give them that chance. He knew exactly what needed to be done.

He cruised past campsite 23, stealing a look in at his RV as he did. As best he could tell, no agents lurked in the darkness. But for how long?

That was anybody's guess. Time was not his friend. And he didn't need Jake's threat of becoming fish meat to cover his tracks.

When he reached campsite 25, he pulled his truck to the shoulder of the gravel road and then killed the engine. He worked to control his breathing as his mind ticked off his exit strategy. He retrieved a set of thin leather gloves from the glove compartment and then, with a jerk, stuffed his hands inside. He disabled the dome light in the cab and, careful not to make unnecessary noise, opened his door.

Once outside, he paused. He gently closed the door with a muted click while his eyes adjusted to the dim moonlight. Behind him, he heard the soft crunch of gravel underfoot. His heart zoomed as the unknown figure approached. He turned around, squinting.

"Good evening," the voice said.

Billy grunted the same in return, not wanting to engage in small talk.

"Nice weather for this time of year, eh?" the man said.

Billy could see the end of the man's cigar glowing in the darkness, although his facial features were nondescript, obscured by the moon's anemic light. "Imagine so," Billy said, relieved this man wasn't with the FBI. Or so he thought. The cigar tipped him off. He figured the FBI didn't pay the average agent enough to smoke cigars.

"Yeah, not cold like we've got it in Toronto, eh?" The man puffed away on this cigar as if he had all the time in the world. "Ever been up north?"

"I'm sorry," Billy said, itching to distance himself as quickly as possible. "It's, um, been a long day." He looked downward. Pale moon or not, he couldn't help but notice the reflection off the man's jet-black, high-gloss shoes. *Odd*, he thought. *Those shoes are for a guy working the beat—not some tourist.* He bit the inside of his lip.

"Yeah, me and the wife are headed to Memphis," the Canadian said, as if he hadn't detected the brush-off. "We're on vacation."

Billy's fingers began to twitch at his side. In his mind he cursed the delay. He had been so pleased that his afternoon went off without a hitch. But now this situation threatened to derail everything he had set in motion.

"Always wanted to see where the King was born, eh?"

"I'm sorry, who?" Billy said, agitated.

"You know . . . the King . . . Elvis, eh?" He stuck the cigar in his mouth.

Hearing the name Elvis, Billy's eyebrows shot up. He sucked in a bucket of air as if he had been sucker-punched. An invisible pair of hands seemed to have seized him by the throat, making it difficult to breathe. Was this guy for real, or was he an agent just playing with his mind? Were there other agents hiding in the trees, gauging his every word, having a laugh at his expense?

After a long moment, in which he regained control of his breathing, Billy managed to say, "Look, I got stuff I gotta do." With that, he turned and then began to walk away, careful not to appear in too much of a hurry as he retraced his steps to his RV, yet half expecting he might need to break into a full run if followed. Billy knew he'd have serious problems outrunning an FBI agent with his bad leg. At least he was more familiar with the camp and could probably shake the guy.

The man called out, "Try to have yourself a nice night."

Relieved that the visitor appeared to be a genuine tourist, Billy slowed his pace to make a more cautious approach. Thirty seconds later the outline of his RV came into view. He stopped under a tall pine tree to listen. He heard the muffled sound of a television cackling away inside a motor home to his right. He could make out the steady hum from traffic on the highway. The only other sound, a dog barking, echoed in the distance.

He stepped away from the shelter of the tree and narrowed the distance between himself and his motor home. Outside the door, he paused to retrieve his key ring from his pocket, careful to avoid unnecessary jingling. He picked out a small, chrome key and then inserted it in the lock. As he worked, his heart thumped so hard against the wall of his chest he was convinced the agents, positioned outside Gloria's pad, could hear it.

At least the key turned without a sound.

Billy reached for the handle and was about to open the door when a new thought flashed through his mind. He couldn't remember whether or not an interior light was triggered to go on automatically when the door opened. If it did, the agents next door would most certainly see the illumination on the window curtains.

He might as well post a billboard announcing his arrival.

Billy swore under his breath. What choice did he have? He had to get inside. He needed just two minutes—if that long. He had to take his chances.

A bead of sweat formed on his forehead as his gloved hand, now moist, pulled the lever down. With a lightning-quick motion he yanked the door open, dashed into the stairwell, and then wrestled the door shut as fast as possible without slamming it. A shot of adrenaline surged through his system as the light doused the stairwell ever so briefly.

Once inside, he paused and caught his breath. He then moved through the darkness to a window facing Gloria's trailer. He peered through a slit in the miniblinds and noticed an agent at the door to Gloria's RV. He was talking to a man inside.

A second later, both men looked in the direction of Billy's RV. Billy didn't know whether they had seen the flash of light, or if the motor home had rocked slightly when he stepped inside. He figured he had precious few seconds to act.

He stooped down and lifted the cushion on the bench sofa. He quickly removed his duffel bag, slinging the strap over his shoulder. Next he snatched up a paper bag that had been stashed inside the oven, and then turned on the gas burners without lighting the pilot. The strong, sour odor of propane gas saturated the air.

Still working in the dark, Billy reached inside the paper bag and removed three bricks of C-4 explosives. He placed one on the floor adjacent to the bedroom door at the rear of the RV. The second he set inside the kitchen sink. The third he placed on the driver's seat.

Billy moved to the doorway, fighting the urge to cough as the fumes replaced the available oxygen. He reached into a cabinet just above the door and retrieved a small gray device. He turned around, placed the homemade unit in the center of the kitchen table, and then pulled up a three-inch antenna.

Three seconds later he was standing outside the RV. He had slipped out as quickly as he had entered with the duffel bag strapped to his back. He walked at a brisk pace, causing pebbles to snap beneath his boots. He reached his pickup truck, slid behind the wheel, shut and locked the doors, and, with a huff, exhaled.

Satisfied that he was clear of immediate danger, Billy yanked off his gloves and started the engine. As he pulled back onto the gravel road, he snatched the cell phone from inside his denim jacket. He punched a phone number into the keypad, pushed the SEND button, and then looked in his rearview mirror.

A few short seconds passed.

A fiery explosion sent fragments of his motor home skyward.

A smile emerged.

What choice did he have? He couldn't drive it away—not with the Feds hot on his trail. He couldn't abandon the RV and leave his fingerprints for them to discover. A complete meltdown was his best, real option to avoid wearing an orange jumpsuit the rest of his life.

With a million bucks flooding the bank each month, a replacement for the RV was the least of his problems. He could buy another one—cash. At the moment, he needed to dodge the agent at the front entrance who, most likely, had been radioed to cut off all exiting traffic.

No problem, he thought, his face scrunched into a sneer.

Billy slipped his truck, with its 4 x 4, into low gear. He headed to the back of the campground and then blazed a trail across the adjacent unplanted cornfield to freedom.

Billy pointed his truck west on the Pennsylvania Turnpike, a toll road, which in his opinion was nothing more than a way for the state to legally pick the pockets of travelers. The New Jersey state line was two exits behind him when Billy's phone chirped a familiar melody. He snatched the phone from inside his coat pocket, holding it without immediately answering the call.

In some ways, even with adrenaline still pumping through his bloodstream from the close call with the FBI, Billy was glad Jake was on the line. He had questions, serious questions, questions Jake would probably have answers for, even if half the time he didn't appreciate the way Jake made him feel for asking.

Billy flipped open his phone on the third ring. "Yo."

"What's the good word? How'd we do today?"

"Um, actually, I couldn't say." Billy cleared his throat. "See—I never made it to the library."

"Because?"

"I had visitors." Billy knew Jake would take time to consider the implications. As the silence filled his earpiece, he glanced in his mirror. Traffic was light and there didn't appear to be anyone on his tail. Still, he wasn't going to take chances. He'd take the next exit.

It was Jake's turn to clear his throat. "Okay. Give me details."

"Hold on." Billy took the Willow Grove exit around to the toll booth and then tossed a fistful of coins into the hand of the attendant. He planned to take local streets toward Horsham, a suburb of Philadelphia. "Sorry. I'm back. Best guess, I'd say they were the Feds."

Another pause on the other end of the phone. Billy switched ears in time to hear Jake say, "Stinkin' FBI. Okay. What else?"

"I'm headed for a fleabag motel tonight. For the life of me I can't figure how they traced me to the RV park—"

Jake swore. "How could you be so stupid, man? You let them find your wheels?"

"Cut it out, Jake," Billy said, snapping. He worked to control the anger in his voice. "I'm not some kind of moron. Just so you know, I blew the camper to kingdom come—just like we planned. They got nothing, I'm tellin' you. No prints. No license plate. Zip."

"Then tell me this," Jake barked. "If you're so brilliant, how'd they find you?"

Billy slowed to a stop at a red light. "First of all, they didn't know my exact location. And they never saw my face." Even as he spoke the words a tinge of doubt surfaced. He wasn't 100 percent positive that the tourist he met was really a tourist. Of course, there was no way he would provide that detail.

"See, I used the computer of an old lady in the camper next to me this morning," Billy said. "Heck, you said it yourself. 'Mix things up.' I had to upload some data. So when the opportunity presented itself, I sent the stuff from her machine. I took the usual precautions. When I got there tonight, they had her place covered. So tell me—" He wanted to add, if *you're* so smart, but thought otherwise. "How'd they get a trace on me?"

Jake considered that for a moment. "I'd say one or more of the anonymous remailers was down. Your electronic trail wasn't completely erased. They're using Carnivore these days, you know. You're lucky to have gotten away, pal. Wait. Hold on a second—you can have the phone when I'm finished." It sounded as if Jake had covered the phone with one hand. "Sorry. The natives are getting restless. One pay phone for fifty guys. Go figure. Anyway, does the word *Carnivore* mean anything to you?"

"No. Not really. Enlighten me." Billy hated the condescending way Jake was talking to him.

"Carnivore is some fancy new tool the FBI has been using since the 9/11 terrorist attacks," Jake said. "A surveillance abuse, if you ask me. Anyway, Carnivore sweeps up all traffic that passes through a computer network. It can pinpoint the location of any machine—anywhere. Down to the phone number where the computer taps into the system."

Billy gripped the wheel tightly. "So . . . sounds like this means we're done, right?"

"Wrong," Jake said. "A minor setback, that's all."

Billy couldn't see how. And the last thing he wanted to do was end up behind bars. "You're unbelievable, man. I'm telling you, the Feds are on to us—it's over, man. We made some serious cash. I say it's not worth the risk and we cut our losses—"

"How about you shut up and just listen to me."

Billy gritted his teeth.

Jake said, "First of all, a couple of million bucks is chump change. I didn't get into this with you for a few measly bucks. I'm tellin' you we can milk this deal—big time. Don't you see, this is the mother of all cash cows? All you have to do is bounce the site to another Web-based server."

Billy laughed. "As if it were that easy. If they traced me today, then they're tracking our Web site. They know—"

"How long are you gonna be stupid?" Jake said. "You're un-stinking-believable. Change the domain name if you like. Call it . . . whatever."

"And what about our fifty thousand subscribers?" Billy shook his head. "You tellin' me we're just gonna walk away from all that cash and start over? A guy goes on-line and can't find MegaFear, then what? We don't get to whack his credit card for twenty bucks anymore."

"So send the people an e-mail . . . from some offshore mailer. Tell them about your new domain name. The point is," Jake spat, "let the Feds try to catch us. We can jump the site around for freaking ever, man. You hear me? That is, as long as we still have the raw video clips, we're in business. Tell me you got the content backed up somewhere. Tell me you didn't blow them up too."

"Lay off, man. The disks are safe." Billy wanted to reach through the phone and smack him. Did Jake really think he'd be so sloppy as to not back stuff up? It was, after all, almost a religious obsession with Billy. That's what his years in the military taught him. Build in redundancies in case of a complication or security breach. Plan for the unexpected.

Each time Billy uploaded video clips to MegaFear.com, he placed a backup DVD, along with the original footage, in his storage unit, one of those pricey, upper-end, security complexes with climate control that provided heat and air conditioning to each unit. He rented a ten-by-twelve space under a false name. Paid cash in advance for the year.

"And another thing," Jake said, interrupting Billy's thoughts. "I've been hitting the books, reading, legal stuff mostly. I'm telling you, you've got nothing to sweat even if the Feds nab you."

"Yeah, right," Billy said, rechecking his mirror at the mention of the FBI. "I'm supposed to believe that?"

"Fine. Don't believe me. Be stupid your whole life."

Billy's jaw tightened. "Okay, I'm listening."

"All right then," Jake said. "As I see it, there's two legal situations to deal with . . . the state level and the Feds."

"Uh-huh."

"Just let me know if I'm boring you," Jake said curtly.

"I said I'm all ears, man."

Jake cupped the phone, his voice muted. "Do I look like I'm done? Get off my case." A series of rustling sounds followed, and then, "I'm back. Okay, now all fifty states have anti-stalking laws. But—and it's a big *but*—less than a dozen states have made it illegal to stalk by computer. Guess what? Pennsylvania and New Jersey aren't among them. At least not yet. By the time legislation closes that loophole, we'll have all the cash we'll ever need."

Billy managed a smile at that bit of information. "Yeah, but what about the Feds?"

"I'm getting there. See, under Title 18 U.S.C. 8751c to be exact, cyber-stalking at the federal level is a crime. I say big deal. The fine maxes out at $250,000—which we make every week. So that's no biggie."

"Yeah. But what about jail time?" Billy scratched the side of his un-shaven face.

Jake laughed. "Again, no biggie. At the most we're talking no more than five years in the pen. Probably get off in six months for good behavior."

"I don't know—"

"Hang with me here," Jake said. "The law says you got to threaten or harass the victim with the computer—and you don't do that, do you?"

"No. I'm their best buddy."

"Exactly. And, you just happen to introduce them to their Maker," Jake said with a chuckle. "That's a whole different drill, of course. The way I see it, as long as you keep yourself invisible, you're gonna be fine. Tell me that isn't worth millions."

Billy pulled into the parking lot of the motel while Jake finished talking. The neon Vacancy sign bounced a pinkish light off the hood of his truck. He shut off the engine.

"Listen, Jake," Billy said, itching to end the conversation. "That's all good. Don't worry, I'm still in the game. But I got stuff I gotta do for tomorrow. You know, with the limo and all."

"Yeah, I think that's one of your more inventive ideas," Jake said, his tone less combative. "Hey, if I were you, I'd use the quarry this time, you know, when you're done filming."

"Sure, the quarry. Anyway, I'm gonna be busy all day," Billy said. "Might buy a new RV. Got to bounce the Web site. Got that prom thing. So we'll talk, um, maybe Saturday. Cool?"

"All right, man," Jake said. "Hey, before you go, tell me—what's this clip called?"

Billy wedged the phone between his chin and left shoulder, and then cracked his knuckles. His lips formed a thin smile.

"I was thinking, uh, something like, 'The Last Dance.'"

Ping-Pong was the pastime of choice in the Adams house. Jodi was above average at the sport, even had her own customized paddle designed to maximize power while balancing her spin control. Her dad, Jack, played in a semipro league, which accounted for the professional table—an inch-thick, blue-top Stiga used during the winter Olympics. They'd bought it at an auction several years back.

Kat, about to lose a best-of-three match to Jodi, placed a hand on the table to leverage her slam. The ball, a Halex Four Star, clipped the corner of the table. "Yes!" Kat shouted, raising her hands above her head.

"Hey," Jodi said, having failed to return the ball, "that point doesn't count."

"In your dreams," Kat retorted, tapping her paddle against her left hand. "Why not?"

"You can't put your hand on the table," Jodi said, retrieving the ball from the corner of the room.

"Says who?"

Jodi stood up, ball in hand. "House rules."

"That's not fair—"

"Oh, so you're, like, the fairness police now, hmm?" Jodi tossed Kat the ball. "Tell you what. Just take your turn over."

"Whatever," Kat said. She served again, but plowed the ball into the net. "I still say you're cheating me." She threw the ball at Jodi.

"Ooh, getting testy, are we?" Jodi teased with a smile. She worked her best top spin on the serve. Kat drove the ball into the ceiling. "That's point," Jodi said, laying her paddle on the table. "How about a rematch?"

Kat laid down her paddle, too, and then checked her watch. "Maybe another time. See, actually, before Heather gets here, I wanna ask you a question."

Heather, Jodi knew, planned to spend the night again, but she'd called to say she was running late. Jodi nodded. "Sure thing. Let's grab something to drink—maybe a snack. Sound good?"

"I'm with you." Kat followed Jodi to the kitchen.

"What's your poison?" Jodi asked, holding open the refrigerator door. "We've got water . . . water . . . oh, and there's water."

Kat straddled a barstool at the counter. "Hmm. Tough choice . . . I'll try the water."

Jodi snagged two bottled waters, some fresh vegetables on a plate, and the ranch dip. She set the items on the counter. "So what's up?"

"Well, I've been really struggling with whether to see my dad or not. Honestly, like, do you think I should go see him, you know, in prison?" Kat said.

Jodi twisted her bottle open, drank deeply, and then wiped her mouth with a napkin. "Well, if my dad were standing here, he'd ask you what you'd hope to accomplish—you know, what's the point of connecting with him?"

Kat nibbled on the end of a carrot stick. "Gosh, I just feel the need to see him, now that everything is so, like, new, you know." She took another bite. "Me being a Christian and all."

Jodi hovered over the veggie plate and settled on a cucumber slice. "That's good, but what's, um, the purpose?"

Kat drank some water. "Well, I feel a peace I've never experienced before and . . . let's just say if there's anybody who needs Jesus big time, it's my dad!"

"So you hope he'll get right with God?" Jodi asked.

"Yeah. I guess that's it—and maybe get an apology, I don't know, for all the stuff in the past." She shrugged. "Or maybe I just need to forgive him to his face."

Jodi's dad appeared in the kitchen from the hallway carrying a bag of trash and then disappeared out the kitchen door.

"Kat, you mind if we ask my dad?"

"Go for it."

Jack returned, empty-handed. "Hey girls. Can I get you anything? Maybe some water?"

"Nice, Dad," Jodi said, holding up her bottle.

"Sorry about the slim pickings," he said. "Mom's going shopping tomorrow."

"Hey, Dad, what do you think?" Jodi said.

"About what?"

"Kat's thinking about seeing her dad—"

"He's in, um, prison over in Jersey." Kat looked down at her feet for an instant. "I haven't seen him in a couple of years. He was a serious jerk—"

"To say the least," Jodi affirmed, "but we don't have to go into details. Anyway, now that Kat's a believer, she's thinking this might be a good time to, like, be an example to him."

Jack listened, rubbing his chin with his right hand. "You know what, Kat? I think your desire to pursue a man who hurt you so deeply is a sign that God is at work in your life."

"Really?" Kat leaned her head to one side.

"I do," Jack said. "But that doesn't mean things will be easy, or that he'll care about your desire to please the Lord with your life. In fact, do you mind if I read you something?"

"Please do, Mr. Adams," Kat said.

Jodi reached for the family Bible. "Here you go, Dad."

"Thanks." He opened to the New Testament. "Funny, I just came across this in my devotions today."

Jodi gave Kat a wink.

"Luke 21:16–19. Wish I had my glasses with me," Jack muttered, holding the pages at arm's length. "It says, 'You will be betrayed even by parents, brothers, relatives and friends, and they will put some of you to death. All men will hate you because of me. But not a hair of your head will perish. By standing firm you will gain life.'"

He closed the Bible, his forefinger still in the page. "Jesus knows what you've been through, Kat. He was betrayed too. By his closest friends. In fact, at one point even his brothers and his mother thought he was kind of off his rocker."

"Wow, I didn't know that," Kat said.

"Jesus understands your pain because he experienced a pain far greater. My point is that, sure, you should go," Jack said. "But listen, Kat. Don't be discouraged or lose hope if your dad rejects you again or tries to wound you with his words."

"Gosh, Jodi"—Kat reached across the counter to tap her on the hand—"your dad should be, like, a preacher."

Jodi laughed. "I agree; he'd be awesome," she said, giving him a side hug. "I say we pray for your dad, Kat."

"You know, there was a time—," Jack started to say when the doorbell sprang to life, cutting him off.

"That's got to be Heather," Jodi said. "I'll get it." Jodi dashed out of the room. Thirty seconds later she walked in with Heather at her side.

"Hey Kat . . . Hey Mr. Adams," Heather said with a wave. "Thanks for having me over again." She dropped her bag at her feet. Heather turned to Jodi, squeezing her arm as she spoke. "Can you believe tomorrow's the big day? I'm so-o-o stinking excited! I can't stand it."

"Yeah, and there's only half a day of school—you gotta love that," Kat added. "So what time's Mr. Wonderful picking you up?"

Heather stole a tentative glance in Jack's direction. "Um, five o'clock . . . at my place."

Jack started to walk toward the family room but stopped and turned around. "Hey, Jodi? Your mom and I just had a talk, and I have something kind of important to say. Let's have a seat in the den for a second. You guys mind?"

The girls exchanged a look.

"Dad, as if you need to ask," Jodi said. The girls took a seat together on the beige sofa. Jack grabbed a stool and sat facing them.

"Well, for starters, I owe each of you an apology."

"Huh, Dad? For what?"

"I've come to see how wrong I was to agree to your meeting that guy this morning," Jack said, his hands cupped together. "I'm afraid I didn't want to disappoint you, Heather. You seemed so set on meeting him. What's his name?"

"Um, it's John Knox," Heather said. "And that's okay."

"I figured it would be safe for you to meet John, especially with both of you around." Jack nodded toward Jodi and then Kat.

Heather laughed. "Well, actually, Mr. Adams, he didn't make it, so we just hung out."

Jack gave her a knowing look. "I know. What you don't know is that I was outside in my car—in the parking lot the whole time—just to make sure you'd be all right."

"Dad!" Jodi shrieked. "I'm so sure—"

Heather cut her off. "Hold on, Jodi. Mr. Adams? You really did that? For me?"

He nodded. "We really do care about you, Heather."

She twirled several strands of hair together. After a moment, she said, "That's so cool, I mean, you took time off work and all—I can't get over that. I don't think even my own dad would have done that. Thank you so much!"

"Well, we're not your parents," he said. He shifted his weight on the edge of the stool, leaning more directly toward Heather. "And you're not our daughter. But because we consider you one of the family, it wouldn't be fair if I didn't say what my wife and I honestly think about all this."

Heather crossed her legs. "I can totally see that. Let me guess—you probably agree with Jodi that I shouldn't go with John tomorrow, am I right?"

"That would be putting it nicely," he said. "Heather, this is serious stuff." He rubbed the palms of his hands together before folding them. "I don't want to sound uptight, but I—we—feel strongly that you'd be making a dangerous mistake to go through with this."

Heather looked away.

"I don't mean to put you on the spot," Jack said softly. "That's the honest truth."

Jodi thought she saw Heather's eyes begin to tear up. "Um, Dad, it's getting kind of late—"

Heather dabbed at the corners of her eyes. "No, it's okay, Jodi. Really it is. I . . . I just don't think anybody understands how wonderful John really is."

Jack cleared his throat. "Listen, Heather. I can't stop you from doing this, even though I'd like to. So here, at least look at this." He withdrew several folded pages from his back pocket and then handed them to her.

"That's a partial transcript," he said. "I downloaded it from the *Oprah* show. She did a special on cyberstalkers. Read it, and maybe you'll understand where we're coming from."

"Thanks," Heather said. "But let's say I still go. What if I took my AOL Instant Messenger with me?"

Jack chuckled. "Hold on a minute. Remember, I'm a media-challenged adult who hasn't figured out how to use the speed dial on his cell phone."

Everybody laughed.

"As it is," Jack said, "I can barely find my way around the Internet. What are you talking about?"

Heather reached into her bag. The device was the size of a pager. "See?" she said, handing it to him. "My dad gave it to me before he left on this trip. It's got a little keyboard and a screen, and it's connected to the Web so I'd be able to stay in touch."

Kat looked skeptical. "Forgive me, but I need to ask the dumb question, Why not just take your cell phone?"

"I—" Heather stopped midsentence. "Yeah, I guess so."

Jack shook his head. "Read the transcript. Please? These cyberstalkers come armed with knives, ropes, guns . . . I'd say a cell phone is no match against these guys."

Nobody spoke for a minute.

"Well, let's say I read this and, um, change my mind," Heather said, rolling the pages into a tube in her hand. "So what now? How do I get out of this, you know, at the last minute?"

"Call him—," Jack Adams began, then stopped. "You do have his phone number, right?"

"Um, I don't. Wait a minute." Heather hooked her hair over her right ear. "I know that sounds crazy but, see, we talk all the time—on the Internet."

"Tell you what," Jack said. "If you can't reach him tonight or after school by e-mail, then I'll go with you to meet him. I'll just inform him the date's been called off—that is, if you'd like."

Heather nodded slowly. "I see."

"Hey, and here's an idea," Jack offered. "Tomorrow, why don't you girls dress up anyway, go to a fancy restaurant and a movie. It'll be my treat. How's that sound?"

The girls exchanged another look and a series of shrugs.

"Dad . . . as long as it's something fancier than Chuck E. Cheese."

"It's a deal," Jack said with a laugh. "Now, if you'll excuse me, I'm heading to bed. See you in the morning." He stood and left the room.

"What are you gonna do, Heather?" Kat asked.

"I'll read this," she said, holding up the rolled paper. "And, um, I'll pray about it, too." Heather pulled her hair back into a loose ponytail, and then said just above a whisper, "What a mess."

"Oh my gosh," Jodi said. "Speaking of prayer, I almost forgot. We were gonna pray for your dad, Kat. What's his name anyway?"

"It's Jake," Kat said. "Jake Koffman."

The FBI Field Office, a large, functional space on the fifth floor of a mostly vacant office building, was outfitted with a maze of gray-metal cubicles. The briefing room, a small open space, contained folding chairs, a dry-erase board, and an oversized map of downtown Philadelphia. The floor-to-ceiling windows revealed an unobstructed view of the statue of William Penn perched atop the City Hall Building one block away.

Dwayne and five other field agents sat in the folding chairs. The smell of smoke, burnt plastic, and fried rubber lingered in the air. Most of the agents were singed around the edges. Several men, having been treated for minor wounds, sported a patchwork of bandages, gauze pads, and white medical tape.

"People—would someone please tell me what happened out there tonight?" Agent Nick Steele leaned against a folding table, jaw flexed, arms folded, his blue shirtsleeves pushed up to the elbows. His side arm, holstered in a black shoulder strap, hung to his left side.

Nobody spoke for a long minute.

Dwayne Whitmore, holding a notepad in one hand, rested his arms on his legs. "Sir, we thought we had the dude. We traced his transmission from"—he paused to check his notes—"the laptop of a Ronnie and Gloria Mason."

"I'm listening," Nick said. He reached for his cup of coffee.

Dwayne straightened up. "We didn't have much time to plan and execute this operation, as you know, sir."

"Go on." Nick nursed his beverage.

"We arrived just after seven," Dwayne said. He scratched the back of his head. "I sent two teams, Frank and Steve, Tom and Hank, with the warrant to pay a visit to the Masons' trailer. Tom and Hank were stationed outside. Frank and Steve went inside. They examined the laptop for prints and the hard drive for evidence—"

"And let me guess, you found nothing, right?" Nick said, looking at Frank and Steve.

"No prints besides those of the owners," said Frank.

"Laptop gave us nothing," Steve said. "It's got a built-in zip drive probably used to send the files."

"A nice couple," Frank added. "Sure don't fit the profile of cyberstalkers. But anything's possible, I imagine."

The room fell silent again.

"I was at the front office with Gene examining the guest register and questioning the owners," Dwayne said after a moment. "Nothing unusual there—at least that we could discover with the time we had. I mean, the park was at maximum capacity. No way even Superman could run down that list before the explosion—"

"Don't get defensive, Dwayne," Nick said. "I'm not looking to pin the blame on anybody tonight. We're all on the same team—let's keep it that way. And frankly," he pointed out, taking another sip of coffee, "we're fortunate nobody was seriously hurt. What else?"

Frank spoke. "Sir, Gloria Mason mentioned that another guest, a man, had helped her that morning fix her e-mail program."

Nick rubbed his temples. "She give you a name?"

"Yes, sir," Frank said. "Claimed it was Elvis—if you can believe that. Didn't know his last name."

"She give a description?"

"A little fuzzy on that score," Frank said. "After the explosion, I joined the other agents to secure the area. The Masons were real shook up. About all Gloria could remember was that this Elvis character had dark hair, maybe black, no facial hair, wore glasses—she thinks they might have been tinted red—and that he walked with a limp."

Steve jumped in. "You're forgetting something. Elvis—or whoever—owned the RV that exploded."

Nick took in the information without comment. He scanned the tired faces of the agents. They each had some field experience, he knew. But behind the keyboard was where they really shone. Indeed, a more experienced field team was appropriate in this situation, but Nick was told the Bureau had already committed too many human assets to the war on terrorism.

"Sir," Dwayne said, "I hate to say it, but the perp got away clean. The dude just vanished."

Nick stood to his full height. "Actually, men, that's where you're wrong."

"But—," Dwayne started to say.

Nick pulled a cigar from his front pocket and waved him off. He bit down on the stogie without lighting it. "In fact, I had a nice little chat with the suspect in the parking lot myself."

Dwayne was halfway out of his chair. "You let him get away? I don't get it. Why didn't you throw his sorry butt in jail?"

"Sit down, please," Nick said, the cigar stuffed in one side of his mouth as he spoke. "If you haven't figured it out by now, the law isn't on our side. We've got the burden of proof, and, Dwayne, we don't have enough on this Elvis character to do more than get him a slap on the wrist."

"Man, with all due respect, what are you talking about? You showed me the guy's Web site—"

"Dwayne, we don't know if those images are real, do we?"

"But—"

The men stared at each other.

"I ain't into horror, but I'd say they're real." Dwayne folded his arms.

"Let's say I agree. Let's say we've got ourselves a bona fide sadistic cyberstalker who has made a cottage industry out of selling fear," Nick said. "What's more, he's a traveler who terrorizes his victims on film."

"Uh-huh. I'm with you."

Nick lit a cigar, rolling it between his thumb and forefinger as the flame roasted the end of the tobacco. A cloud of smoke encircled his bald head, like the ring around Saturn. "If I had arrested him tonight, tell me, where's the hard evidence that links him to the creation of those images?"

Dwayne tilted his head. "We don't have any, but—"

"My point exactly," Nick said. "With what we've got, Elvis, or whatever-his-real-name-is, would be back on the streets in less than twenty-four hours."

Frank rocked back on the hind legs of his folding chair. "So we're back to square one, boss?"

Nick waited until all eyes were on him. "No, Frank. First, I got a decent look at the man's features. He couldn't wear his tinted glasses because it was too dark. Second, we know he's driving a black, late-model Nissan Frontier pickup truck with Jersey plates."

Dwayne whistled.

Nick folded his arms and held the cigar within reach of his lips. "Oh, one more thing. I took the liberty of placing a tracking device under the dash of his pickup truck while he was blowing up his RV."

Dwayne's mouth dropped open. "How'd you—"

"I didn't," Nick said. "There wasn't time to get a warrant. At the moment, based on the signal picked up with our Global Positioning satellite, I'd say our man plans to spend the night at the Vagabond Inn in Horsham."

"I'm there," Dwayne said, now standing.

Nick's jaw tightened. "Listen, men. Elvis is to be considered armed and dangerous. I want him under surveillance, but give him lots of rope. Dwayne—"

"Sir?"

"I want one team here to track any activity related to the Web site."

"Done." Dwayne nodded toward Frank and Steve.

"I want the other two teams to take turns on his tail."

"Gene and I will do the overnight," Dwight said, yawning. "Tom and Hank will relieve us at 0700."

Nick blew out a cloud of smoke. "Remember, we've got the eye-in-the-sky tracking his truck, so there's no need to get too close. I don't want our cover blown on this."

Dwayne and Gene started for the door.

"One more thing," Nick said. "I've been bustin' bad guys for more years than I care to remember. After a while, you can get kinda calloused. But I'm telling you, this schmo takes the cake—the cyberstalking, the kidnapping, the trauma, and the audacity to sell it. Stay sharp—I want 'Elvis' singin' 'Jailhouse Rock' in the slammer for the rest of his sorry life."

Billy couldn't fall asleep. He stole a look at the readout on the cheap alarm clock by his bed for the hundredth time, or so it seemed. Just after one o'clock. He swore at how slowly time was moving. His leg hurt. His temples pounded with the intensity of dueling jackhammers. Even his hair hurt.

At midnight, he had decided to take a shower to help him relax. But the anemic flow trickling out of the rusted chrome fixture failed to produce hot water. The towels, he discovered, weren't much better. He guessed they were just larger than a washcloth and thin enough to see through in places. Dried-off as best as was possible, Billy had pulled on the same underwear and clothing. It wasn't as if he'd had time to pack an overnight bag. Everything got fried along with the RV.

After the miserable shower, his shirt sticking to the moisture on his back, he tried the TV. The relic sat on a flimsy-looking shelf mounted to the wall. With no remote control and just three channels producing more static than signal, he was discouraged from bothering with the box.

He turned, then walked across the thin, tacky carpet to adjust the air conditioner, a wall unit mounted above the door. With a flick of the switch, the unit managed to rattle, cough, and vibrate, while providing little relief from the stuffiness. He smacked the thing off.

Billy cursed his decision to stay in this rathole. About the only item in the room that appeared to him as new, even unused, was the Gideon Bible in the bedside drawer. He would have stayed at the Hampton Inn, maybe the Marriott or Courtyard, but, as he'd learned from the kid manning the check-in, the Willow Grove Naval Air Station was having their graduation ceremonies that weekend. All the newer hotels had been booked months ago. Yes, he should be glad he'd found anything.

What did he expect for $29.99?

Evidently, fresh air wasn't included in the price. He tried the front window but it was jammed. Layers of dust and neglect rendered it useless. With some effort, he opened the rear window. It provided a view of the alley behind the motel, which apparently served as the final resting place for an assortment of broken bottles, a collection of used tires, an upside-down shopping cart, and a mass of discarded papers.

At least the air was crisp. He inhaled as his gaze drifted toward the half-moon overhead. His brain felt as if it were on the verge of an explosion as he alternately reflected on last night's meltdown and tomorrow's checklist.

He had to lie down.

Billy collapsed into the bed; a hammock would have offered more comfort. He looked at the clock again. In the darkness, the red digital readout glowed softly. He shifted the pillows under his neck and kicked the tattered bedspread onto the floor.

How?

How'd they find him?

Who found him?

Probably the FBI, but he didn't know for sure. In the back of his mind, something about the shoes worn by the Canadian visitor bothered him. He recalled how completely out of place they seemed. He remembered they were too polished, too rounded at the edges. Had to be the FBI.

Were they on his trail—maybe outside his door even now?

He covered his head with a pillow.

He needed sleep. He needed to plan. He needed to go on-line. That, however, was out of the question. The moment he'd arrived he noticed the black rotary-dial phone positioned by the bed. He discovered the motel didn't provide touch-tone service. With the library closed hours ago, Billy had no way to connect to the Internet. Of all the bad luck.

Maybe he should postpone tomorrow's planned encounter. It wouldn't have been the first time plans were aborted. He'd had to bail in the past, so why not now? He could wait until the heat cooled off. On the other hand, the prom angle had so many delicious possibilities. If he passed on this occasion, he'd have to wait a full year for the prom to roll around again.

He sat upright in bed. No. Nothing would stop him. Not even the FBI. She would be, after all, decked out in a beautiful dress—maybe with matching high heels. Her hair and nails would be perfect. The contrast to the fear on her face when she realized she wasn't going to the prom after all would be—*intense.*

That's what people loved about MegaFear.com.

Surely subscribers would line up to pay an extra fee for a download of the video file. He could almost see the money growing in the offshore account. He licked his lips and then realized how thirsty he had become.

His duffel bag, with its stash of lethal weapons, lay on the floor within easy reach of his bed. He reached inside, snatched up the 9mm, rose from the bed, and then tucked the gun in his waistband as he peered out the front window before opening the door. The vending machines he had noticed earlier were outside and to the left of his door.

Billy cracked the door open, an inch at first. He gripped the doorknob with his gloved hand, waited, and then stepped outside. He was surprised to see every parking slot filled. A buzzing sound from the Vagabond Inn sign, probably an electrical wire ready to burst, he thought, filled the air with its continuous low-pitched whine. Other than the droning sign, an occasional car passing on the main drag, and a lone cricket rubbing its legs together, the night air was quiet.

Halfway to the Coke machine, a strange feeling came over him. He sensed that a set of eyes were drilling a hole in the back of his head. He pretended to stretch as he stole a look across the parking lot. Nothing—at least that he could see without being too obvious.

He took several more steps toward the vending area when he heard a door open behind him. He reached for the pistol's grip, but released his hold when sounds of laughter broke the silence. He turned in time to see a couple staggering out, kissing.

Billy breathed again and faced the machine. He stuffed change in the slot, a task made more difficult with his gloves, and then snapped up his beverage. As he returned to his room, his military training kicked in. His eyes bounced from building to building, car to car, window to window. A soft tingling sensation, like the wings of a butterfly, fluttered in his ears with each unfamiliar sound.

His head jerked up as a milk truck rumbled down the main road, its headlights on high beam. From the corner of his eye, a glint of light, brief that it was, caught his attention.

There it was again. To his left. Across the street.

He pretended to fumble with his room key, using the moments to steal a better look. Two men in an unmarked car. With binoculars—the headlights must have reflected off the lenses, he thought.

"What do we have here?" Billy said under his breath.

Once inside, lights still off, he stood with his back to the door. Billy knew he had three immediate problems. Topping the list was the fact he had been followed. Now he had to find a way to shake the tail. But how? He couldn't drive away. Too obvious. He couldn't walk out the front door and wait for a cab.

Then again, thankful the motor lodge was one story, he could leave through the rear window, walk behind the motel under the cover of darkness, and make his way in the shadows to the 7-Eleven store he'd seen three blocks away.

He would call ahead on a disposable cell phone to have a taxi waiting. He kept several phones in his bag for emergencies. They were wonderfully inexpensive and absolutely necessary. He would toss the thing away just in case the Feds were tracing cell transmissions.

That decided, his second priority was to sanitize the room before leaving. He couldn't afford to have his fingerprints lurking behind. He might as well send the FBI a postcard with his real name and photo ID.

He was tempted to blow up the room. But such spectacular events, by their nature, drew unwanted attention. Last night, torching the RV couldn't be avoided. Then again, a fire in a dive like this wouldn't be that unusual. He could slip a lit cigarette into the mattress. It would smolder away for hours until it built up a good head of steam. The room would be engulfed in flames.

He smiled at the thought, but quickly dismissed the option.

He finished his Coke, tossed it out the back window, and then grabbed a washcloth. Even though he had worn his gloves most of the time in the room, he couldn't be completely sure he didn't leave a lone fingerprint somewhere.

In the dark, he worked quickly to wipe the door handle, the air conditioner, the clock—although he wasn't sure he had even touched it, the front and rear window jambs, the TV, the shower stall, and the phone.

Satisfied, his third challenge was much more difficult to deal with: how to dispose of his truck. Fingerprints aside, the pickup contained secrets that, if discovered, would put him away for life. He was fairly confident that DNA evidence linking him to certain missing persons could probably be uncovered on the bed liner.

Again, he knew there wasn't anything that a good fire couldn't hide. But he was fresh out of C-4. He could drive the truck into the quarry, but it was too far and he'd have no way back—not to mention the FBI escort he would most likely have. He would think of something—tomorrow.

Billy checked the time: almost three. It was now or never. He carefully lowered his bag out the rear window, and then climbed out after it where he vanished into the darkness.

CHAPTER 13 ✦ FRIDAY, 6:51 A.M.

The early morning sun, its rays streaking through the kitchen window, bathed the breakfast table in a warm glow. Jodi reached for her orange juice and quietly surveyed the faces of her friends over the rim of her glass.

Kat was eating as if she hadn't had a decent meal in weeks. Of course, Kat's mom never cooked, which might explain her enthusiasm over a homemade meal. Heather was another story. She poked at her pancakes without conviction.

Jodi set down her glass. "Thanks for making breakfast, Mom," she said, breaking the silence that hung like a low cloud over the table.

"Yeah, it's really good," Kat said, digging into her stack of pancakes.

"You're quite welcome," Jodi's mom said over her shoulder as she disappeared down the hall.

Jodi knew if anybody was *not* a morning person, it'd be Kat. Yet today, Kat, not Heather, seemed alert and ready to talk. Jodi figured Kat was deferring to Heather's somber mood.

More silence.

Jodi reached for the syrup. "So, what's up, Heather?"

Heather put down her fork. "Don't pretend you don't know."

"Ouch!" Kat said.

"Come on, Heather—"

Heather crossed her arms and then slumped against the back of her chair. "Why don't you both just keep out of my head."

"This is about John, isn't it?" Jodi said after a moment.

Heather blinked.

"Listen, I'm, um, sorry for you that John wasn't on-line last night," Jodi said, hooking her hair over her right ear. "I know how much you wanted to talk things out with him."

"Don't pretend you care about John, because you don't." Heather looked away.

"Gosh, Heather. Give us a break here," Kat said, holding her fork midair above her plate. "Okay, I admit it. I was beginning to change my mind that maybe things were cool after you got those flowers and note from John. But"—she put down her fork—"after what Jodi's dad said last night, I'm back to thinking that going to the prom with a virtual stranger is a great way to get screwed up. That doesn't mean you have to be all uptight."

Heather turned to Kat. "What do you know about—"

"Hello? I'm, like, an expert at being screwed up, remember?" Kat said with a laugh.

"She's got you there," Jodi said.

Heather smiled.

Jodi looked at the clock on the wall. She knew they had to leave soon to be on time for school. "So, like, why do you think it's so hard to let him go, Heather?"

"Yeah," Kat chimed in. "There'll be other cool guys—"

"I can see neither of you are gonna leave it alone," Heather said. She shifted in her seat. "Can't you see . . . this was only supposed to be one of the best days of the year, you know? I mean—do you have any idea how much I've been looking forward to this day?"

Heather looked at Jodi and then Kat. "I don't mean just going with John—that's a big part of it for sure. But I am, after all, on the prom committee. This is only *the* event of the semester. I can't just not show up."

Kat started to say something, but Jodi gave her the evil eye so Heather would keep talking.

"I mean, I had my day all planned out, too," Heather said. "You know how I have study hall fourth period?"

Jodi nodded.

"Since today's a half day, I was going to cut out a little early, pick up my dress at the cleaners—"

"What? I thought you bought a new one?"

"I did. It's being altered," Heather explained.

"Oh, you scared me," Jodi said. "For a second, I thought you were using an old dress."

"Right," Heather said. "Anyway, I was gonna do my nails at one . . . my hair at two . . . and still have plenty of time to get ready before John picked me up. Everything was gonna be just perfect."

"I imagine so," Jodi said, still skeptical. She wiped her hands on a napkin. "But did you read that stuff my dad gave you last night?"

"Sure, I read it."

"So did I," Kat said, swallowing. "For me, um, I still can't get over the part where that lady was talking about her daughter and how the girl arranged to meet that pervert. Now she's vanished"—Kat snapped her fingers—"like, she's completely gone. They still haven't found her six months later."

Heather sighed. "I think my situation is totally different."

"Like how?" Kat asked.

"For starters, I'm seventeen, not fourteen," Heather said.

"As if that makes a big difference," Kat said.

Jodi reached over and playfully punched Kat in the shoulder. "Let her talk."

"My point is, I'm not naive," Heather said. "Another difference is that John's never talked about having sex, never asked for a picture of me in some sexy pose, never said anything about wanting me to have his baby . . ."

Jodi and Kat laughed.

"John's a real gentleman," Heather continued. "And, like I've said a hundred times, he's a Christian, too."

"Things aren't always what they appear to be, Heather, you know that," Jodi said.

Heather stood abruptly. "Why don't you let me be the judge of that?

Besides, I can't just stand John up—after all, he's planned a limo and all."

"Come on, Heather, I . . . well, I heard what you said, but I don't want to be sitting here tomorrow reading about you in the newspaper, you know?" Jodi said. "There are a lot of sickos out there. Maybe you should, like, pray about it some more."

"All right already, Jodi," Heather said stiffly. "Look, I gotta get going—"

"I didn't mean to offend you."

"Uh-huh."

Jodi felt sure Heather wanted to bite her head off. "Oh . . . remember, if things were to change, you know, about going with John, um, my dad's willing to . . . to . . ."

"Bail me out?"

"He *was* sweet to offer," Kat said. "I wish I had a dad like him."

"Whatever." Heather reached for her purse and overnight bag.

"Listen, Heather," Jodi said. "If you change your mind, Kat and I are definitely up for tagging along with you to the prom, aren't we, Kat?"

Kat's eyes widened. "Um, right." She lowered her voice and added, "I thought your dad was gonna treat for dinner and a movie?"

Jodi shrugged. "Dinner . . . the prom . . . either way. My point is, Heather, you don't *have* to go with John. And the three of us can still have a blast together."

Heather pulled her keys out of her pocket. "Okay, *Dear Abby*, since you're so full of advice, here's my question: What do I tell all my friends tonight—who can't wait to meet John—if I show up with you and Kat instead of him? Did you think of *that?*"

Jodi held her tongue, watching as Heather turned and walked away in a huff. She heard the front door close with a forceful thump and then turned to Kat. "You know what? I think we ought to pray for her."

"Okay," Kat said.

"Hey, you wanna start?"

"Me? I'm still kinda new at all this—"

"Kat, as if that matters!" Jodi smiled. "God's not impressed by our words. He cares what's in here." She pointed toward her heart. "Go on . . . give it a try."

Kat's eyebrows shot up. "Okay—I guess," she said, folding her hands and bowing her head. "Um, Jesus, look, Jodi and I just want to say we're, like, really concerned about our friend Heather . . . and . . . I—we—pray that she would, um, decide not to go tonight with that guy. Keep her safe always. Amen."

Kat looked up at Jodi. "How was that?"

Jodi wiped dampness from her eyes.

"That bad, huh?" Kat said, her forehead crumpled in a knot.

Jodi laughed. "Do you have any idea how wonderful it is to hear you pray? You did great. I'm serious!"

Kat's face brightened.

"Oh, Kat, I've been meaning to ask you all morning," Jodi said, reaching over to squeeze Kat's hand. "I wanted to know if you feel like seeing your dad today, maybe, like, after school."

Kat laughed. "I should be asking you that question."

"How's that?"

"Let's just say Dad's no saint," Kat said, the sunlight dancing off an earring. "Me? Yeah, I think today's good—sure beats the heck out of watching Heather get her nails done!"

They laughed.

Kat said, "Okay, so let's meet in the parking lot at school, say, twelve-fifteen-ish?"

"Deal." Jodi made a mental note of the time. "And pray Heather makes the right decision."

"Hey, we could always break her legs so she can't go—"

Jodi punched her in the arm. "*Now* who's the psycho?"

CHAPTER 14 ✳ FRIDAY, 7:00 A.M.

Agent Dwayne Whitmore and his partner, Gene, still parked across from the Vagabond Inn, sat low in the front seat of their Bureau-issued, charcoal brown Ford Taurus. The driver's and passenger's side windows were rolled down, permitting a soft breeze to waltz through the car. Dwayne sat behind the wheel. He checked his watch.

"Seven-oh-one. They're officially late."

Hank appeared almost out of nowhere at Dwayne's window.

"Sleeping on the job?"

Dwayne turned his head to the left and produced a gaping yawn. "Man, I saw you coming a mile away." He stretched his arms out in front of him, fingers entwined, palms out.

"Here, boss," Hank said. "Brought you some coffee. Black." Hank passed two Styrofoam cups through the window. "That's to keep you guys awake long enough to get home."

"Bless you, my man," Dwayne said. "I'll make a note of it in my report: kissing up to a superior."

Gene, sitting on the passenger side, leaned over. "Tell me, Hank, where'd you Girl Scouts park?"

Hank nodded in the direction of a berm of tall pine trees. "Tom's got the wheel—yeah, I'd say he's working on his arts 'n' crafts as we speak. Probably knitting you a pair of boxers."

"Okay, kids, let's play nice," Dwayne said. He pushed Gene back into his seat.

"Tom and I will take it from here," Hank said. He kept his back toward the motel. "The joint looks packed. Tell me, which room is Elvis in?"

"A-5," Dwayne said without pointing.

Hank scratched his chest. "Any activity with our man?"

Dwayne rubbed the sleep out of his eyes. "Nothing. Hasn't stirred since, what—about one?" He looked at Gene.

"Yeah, he came outside for a Coke or something. It's been quiet ever since."

Hank said, "Get out of here and get some rest. Nothing personal, but you guys look like extras from *The Return of the Walking Dead.*"

Dwayne reached for the ignition when an explosive bang, with the force of a thunderclap, cracked the air. All three men reached for their service revolvers. Hank ducked low beside the car door for cover.

"Hold on," Dwayne said as a small, light-duty tow truck rumbled into view. It rolled to a stop on the side of the road adjacent the motel then belched and backfired again. Dwayne snapped his fingers three times at Gene.

"Binoculars."

Gene retrieved them from the glove compartment and then handed them over.

Dwayne raised the field glasses to his eyes.

"We got an unmarked tow truck . . . The driver's the only occupant . . . He's checking a clipboard . . . There he goes, he's pulling into the Vagabond parking lot . . . He's . . . hold on . . . he's backing up to Elvis's pickup truck. I'd say we got ourselves a situation."

Gene reached for the radio microphone.

"Unnecessary," Dwayne said, waving him off.

"Shouldn't we check in with command?"

"No. We have our orders. Our job is to shadow Elvis—not his truck."

"But he's gonna tow it away—"

"Let him. Dude, we got the GPS bug planted inside," Dwayne said. "It don't matter where Mr. Gearhead tows it. The satellite will have a fix on it."

Hank straightened up. "You want me to talk to the driver? See who sent for it?"

"And give away our cover?" Dwayne said. "Negative. I'd say Elvis doesn't know we're here. How could he? I'll tell you what, Hank. You and Tom get into position to cover the back of the motel in case he plans to run for it, but stay out of view. We're only supposed to shadow Elvis—not get him *all shook up.*"

Hank laughed. "Roger that." He spun around and then headed for his car.

Dwayne handed the binoculars to Gene. "See if you can ID the plates on that tow truck."

Gene squinted. "Pennsylvania plates . . . It's P3T-6X0 but the first digit might be a *B,* and that last digit could be another six, maybe an eight . . . With the dirt it's almost impossible to tell."

"Tell you what," Dwayne said. "Call the numbers in—give them your options—they'll run the tags."

Dwayne put his hands on the steering wheel. His thumbs began to tap away with nervous energy. "Whatcha doing, Elvis? Is a buddy coming to pick you up? Or—let me guess—you put on your blue-suede shoes and called a cab."

CHAPTER 15 ✳ FRIDAY, 7:55 A.M.

The taxi ride cost Billy eighty bucks, a cheap price to pay for his freedom. He had given the driver a hundred-dollar bill and told him to keep the change. He arrived at the Airport Embassy Suites about three that morning, having called ahead in the cab to verify rooms were available. He had checked in using his Elvis Smith ID. He hated to use that alias with the FBI hot on his tail. He had promised himself he would get a new identity tomorrow—certainly by Saturday.

Once situated in his room, an oversized king bed suite with three working TVs and remote controls, he had placed a call to Otto's Auto Salvage. Otto, he knew, slept in a trailer on the property. Otto wouldn't mind getting a call at that early hour—at least not with the amount of money Billy planned to wave in his direction.

Yes, Otto would send a tow truck to retrieve Billy's pickup.

Yes, it would be delivered to the salvage yard by eight.

Yes, Otto would mash the daylights out of it.

Satisfied with his plan, Billy drifted into a sound sleep.

After devouring the complimentary buffet breakfast, Billy had taken a cab about four miles from the hotel to Otto's Auto Salvage, a sprawling eyesore covering fifty acres, piled high with rusting car parts and skeletons of burned-out car frames. The yard was surrounded by a crusty chain-link fence topped with barbed wire.

He arrived five minutes before eight o'clock, just in time to watch Otto's rickety tow truck, groaning, as it struggled to pull the Nissan into the lot. Otto's son was behind the wheel.

"Morning, Otto," Billy said. He started to walk toward the office, a trailer with dirty glass windows overlooking the yard.

Otto stood on the makeshift deck just outside the office, his back hunched slightly as if the force of gravity was pulling him downward. He stroked his bushy gray beard and shook his head in disbelief.

"Did my boy get the right truck?"

"Sure did." Billy turned around for a final look. For a second, he considered whether he had left anything of value in the truck. No. Everything he needed was in the duffel bag hung over his left shoulder.

"I say, son, I've seen some strange things in my time, but this sure beats 'em all." Otto scratched the top of his head. "You sure you want to go through with this?"

"Positive." As Billy spoke the word, a new thought crossed his mind. Maybe the truck had been bugged. How else did the FBI trace him to the motel last night? He got away clean from the campground. And, come to think of it, if the pickup was bugged, they'd be able to trace him here. The thought sent his heart pounding. His eyes darted toward the entrance, half expecting to see a caravan of agents crashing the place.

Billy looked the man in the eye. "Otto, let's get this done."

Otto whistled at his son. "Go ahead, pull it onto the platform," he said with a wave of his leathery hand.

Billy climbed the steps to the platform and then followed Otto inside the cramped trailer.

"I mean . . . once I press this here button," Otto said, pointing toward a small panel under the middle window, "there's no stopping the Shredder." The old man said the words as if the machine were a living creature.

"Give me the release form. I want it smashed."

"Well, yeah, it's just that your truck is in such fine shape." Otto handed Billy a clipboard with a half sheet of paper under the clip. "Sign right there."

Billy scribbled his name. He walked to the window and scanned the yard for intruders.

Otto tossed the clipboard onto his wooden desk, itself a cluttered junkyard.

"Yeah, I wish I had me a set of wheels that purdy—"

"Crush it, Otto—now. You don't get paid until that truck is pulverized."

"Whoa! Don't get testy on me, son." Otto moved into position. He stroked the bottom end of his beard. "I just want to make sure—"

Billy swore under his breath. "Push the button. I don't got all day."

"Don't say I didn't warn you." He smashed the red button with his thick, calloused forefinger. The Shredder did the rest.

"There. As agreed," Billy said as he peeled five crisp hundred-dollar bills from a wad of cash in his pocket. "And this is to keep your mouth shut."

He counted out five more bills.

Otto whistled. "Son, I don't know a thing."

At least a dozen new car dealerships were located directly across the street from Otto's salvage. Rows of shiny new vehicles, balloons tied to their antennas, lined the road for what seemed like miles in either direction.

After Billy was reasonably certain the coast was clear, he crossed the street carrying his duffel bag. He needed wheels, and he needed them fast. It had to be a 4 x 4, with an off-road package; something besides another truck would be best. And it had to be an automatic. Operating a clutch with his bad leg was out of the question.

At the Nissan dealer, a fully loaded, alpine green XTERRA, with over-sized, road-eating tires, caught his eye.

He paid cash.

CHAPTER 16 ✦ FRIDAY, 12:14 P.M.

Sit down, Dwayne." Nick stood behind his desk, flanked by an American flag on the right. The official FBI seal was mounted on the wall to his left. He motioned to a chair. "Please."

"Listen, Nick, I have no idea how we . . ."

"Botched the operation?" Nick said, finishing Dwayne's sentence. He folded his arms.

Dwayne took a deep breath. "What can I say?"

Nick studied the younger agent, who shifted in his seat like a man waiting on death row. Nick had sat in that same chair years ago. Different dropped ball, same chair.

"Look, Dwayne," Nick said after a minute. He loosened his tie and opened his collar. "I didn't call you in here to read you the riot act."

"Hey, boss, I'm not gonna make excuses," Dwayne said, leaning forward, head down, his arms resting on his legs. "But last night, as I recall, we threw the operation together on the fly. This dude outsmarted us. Or maybe he just had a lucky break. I'm sorry it went down that way."

Nick circled around to the front of his massive desk. He leaned against the edge. "Here, take a good look at this." Nick handed Dwayne a nine-by-twelve enlargement of a photograph.

"Who's this?"

"Let's just say it's an Elvis sighting."

"Now you're blowing my mind," Dwayne said with a whistle. He pored over the image. "How'd you score this picture?"

Nick smiled. "Like you said, sometimes you get a lucky break. I got a call this morning—about eight—from Gloria Mason. I gave her my card last night."

"Oh, yeah. The lady from the RV park."

Nick nodded. "Seems she finally got around to opening a package of film she had developed last week. She's big into hummingbirds. Took a picture of one hovering by the feeder. It's mounted on her awning." Nick pointed. "See—there in the foreground."

"Got it."

"Just our luck, when Gloria snapped the picture, Elvis happened to be outside his vehicle doing whatever he was doing," Nick said. "I can confirm that's the same guy I spoke with last night. The one who fled the scene in the black pickup." Nick cleared his throat and added, "The one who gave you the slip this morning."

"Speaking of that," Dwayne said, "where'd they tow his truck?" He handed the photo back to Nick.

Nick walked around the desk and sat in his high-backed leather chair. "A dumpy salvage outfit by the airport—across from the auto mall."

"I know the place."

"I can only assume by now the truck's a pancake, or torched," Nick said. "Our signal died shortly after eight."

Dwayne looked at the floor, and then at Nick. "What about the soda can? You find any prints?"

"Actually, yes."

"For real?"

"Yes. Even though you rookies lost our primary target," Nick said, leaning back in his seat, "you exhibited a brilliant bit of detective work when you spotted his Coke can behind the motel."

"Oh, that," Dwayne said. "See, things didn't add up. He bought a drink—Gene and I saw that for a fact. When we checked the room after he, uh, like you said, 'gave us the slip,' guess what?"

Nick shrugged.

"No Coke can in the trash, or anywhere for that matter," Dwayne said, a smile filling his face. "Elvis didn't come out the front, so we looked around back. Heck, the can was brand-new. Stood out like a sore thumb next to the old junk."

"Chalk one up for the good guys," Nick said. "We lifted a partial print.

We compared the print and his mug from the photo to the Bureau's database. I had the boys run a full background check. Turns out he's no ordinary loner."

"Hold on. He's ex-CIA? Don't tell me he's one of ours?"

"Close, but thankfully, neither." Nick folded his hands behind his head. "His full name is William T. Bender. Goes by Billy. He sometimes uses the alias 'Elvis Smith.' He's ex-military. Served with the army in Desert Storm. He's skilled in explosives—"

Dwayne nodded. "That explains the RV."

"Right." Nick leaned forward and read from a yellow legal pad. "He's trained in surveillance, intelligence, and computers. No formal education, but tested in the top 5 percent in his unit." Nick looked up from his notes. "He's smart. Probably a little too smart."

"You said he's ex-military. What happened?"

Nick folded his hands on his desk. "Dishonorable discharge. Seems Billy plays rough. A little too rough. And he plays for keeps. He's got a history of violence. Finally got himself discharged when his team leader told him to release a prisoner."

Dwayne scratched his chin.

"Instead of standing down, Billy sliced the prisoner's throat."

Dwayne shook his head. "You thinkin' what I'm thinkin'?"

"That his MegaFear Web site is the real deal?" Nick said.

"Sir, I'd bet on it."

"And I'd agree," Nick said. "But we need proof if we're gonna put him away."

Dwayne made a fist with his right hand and slammed it into his left hand. "Dang, I wish we hadn't lost his trail this morning. Now what?"

Nick ran his hand over the top of his bald head. "For starters, get somebody working the phones. I want every miniwarehouse complex in the city called. See if there's a unit rented to Billy Bender or Elvis Smith. And get names of everyone who paid in cash over the last six months."

"What's the angle?"

"I figure most folks would write a check," Nick said. "Billy, on the other hand, would probably pay in cash to avoid bank records. And so far as we can tell, Billy has no known permanent address. He's got to park his, I don't know, his—*stuff* somewhere. A storage unit is as good a place as any to start looking."

"Man, are you good." Dwayne said, rolling his head from shoulder to shoulder.

Nick ignored the compliment. "Who knows. Maybe we'll get lucky again and find a stash of computer disks, video equipment, files—any or all of which could be the smoking gun we need, as it were. And send two guys to that junkyard," Nick added. He consulted his notes. "Otto's Auto Salvage. Take copies of his photo. See if anybody can ID him."

"Done," Dwayne said. "Hey, he'd need something else to drive, right? We'll flash the picture around the dealerships too."

"You do that," Nick said. "Now get out of here. We need to get a line on Billy before he adds another face to his Web site."

CHAPTER 17 ✳. FRIDAY, 1:04 P.M.

This place gives me the creeps," Kat said, her voice just above a whisper. She and Jodi stood against the back wall of the visitors' room in the New Jersey state prison waiting for Kat's dad to be escorted in. "It's so, um, thrashed, you know? The place is all dark and old."

"You're not serious, are you?" Jodi whispered back. "What did you expect? Martha Stewart Village?"

"And guards everywhere . . . no windows . . . Gosh, it's a regular dungeon," Kat said. "I had no idea." Kat started to fidget with an earring.

Jodi studied Kat's face for a moment. *It's gotta be so hard to know your dad will spend twenty years here,* Jodi thought. "You still wanna do this?"

Kat leaned toward Jodi's ear. "I don't know. Yeah, I guess. I mean, he's got to hate me for squealing on him."

Jodi squeezed her arm. "You did the right thing, Kat."

"That's why I never came to see him before, you know."

"I can see that," Jodi said. "But no matter what he says, just remember why you came today."

Kat's brow crumpled. "Why was that, again?"

Jodi spoke into Kat's ear. "To let him see the change in you . . . and maybe . . . to forgive him for the past."

"You're right." Kat nodded. "Thanks for being such a good friend. So how do I look?"

"Simply awesome," Jodi said, picking a piece of lint off Kat's shoulder.

The girls fell silent.

"You see Heather at school?" Jodi asked, hopeful the change of subject would help Kat pass the time.

"No. How about you?"

"Yeah," Jodi said. "I bumped into her in the hall after third period, I wanna say around eleven-ish."

"Really? Did she change her mind about tonight?"

"She didn't say, exactly." Jodi looked over Kat's shoulder at the guard station. "Actually, she gave me the brush-off. Said she was cutting out early . . . something about prom committee privilege . . . but I'd say she was going to the dry cleaners to pick up her new dress."

Kat considered that for a second. "Really? What makes you think so?"

"The yellow dry-cleaning slip and car keys in her hand kind of tipped me off." Jodi smiled. "Oh, look. To your left. With the guard. Is that him?"

Kat looked over her shoulder. "Um . . . that's him! Oh my gosh—he's lost weight." She turned back to Jodi, her face pale.

A guard approached the girls and then said, "We're ready. Please follow me."

Jodi felt Kat's hand touch the center of her back as they walked to station three. The guard directed them to two folding chairs that were set side by side.

"Miss Koffman," the guard said, motioning her to the right seat. "Miss Adams," he said, directing Jodi to the left chair. As the girls took their places, Kat offered a nervous wave to her dad through the glass partition. "Each of you has a phone so you'll both be able to talk and listen," the guard explained. "I'll be right over there if you need anything." He pointed to the guard station.

"Thanks," they said in unison.

Jodi gave Kat a wink, and then picked up the phone. Kat did the same.

Jake took a cigarette from his pocket, placed it in his mouth and then picked up his phone.

"Um, hey Dad . . . nice to see you," Kat said weakly.

"Who's she?" Jake's eyes narrowed.

"She's, um, my friend, Jodi . . . from school."

Jake's face tightened. He didn't look directly at Jodi.

"Hi, Mr. Koffman," Jodi said, trying to sound natural, as if they weren't surrounded by guards with rifles.

Jake glared at Kat. "Something happen to your mother?"

"No, sir," Kat said. "Mom's fine, I mean, what I see of her. She's not around much—"

"What's this about?" Jake scowled.

Jodi could sense Kat tensing up.

Kat said, "Um, I . . . we—"

Jake cut her off. "This some kind of field trip?"

"No, Dad." Kat clutched the phone with both hands. "I wanted to see you, and Jodi here came along because—"

Jake cut her off. "What am I, an animal at the zoo?" A guard gave Jake a light. He took a sustained drag from his cigarette and then blew out a cloud of smoke. "I'm locked up two years and you never bothered to see your old man."

"I *am* sorry about that . . ."

"Uh-huh." Jake coughed. "You're sorry. I'm sorry. Everybody's sorry. Big deal. So what—I'm supposed to be happy to see the person who put me here?"

Kat shook her head. "That's so not fair—you made choices, Dad . . . Say what you want, but you put yourself here."

"Well, now that we've got that settled," Jake said, "I guess I'll get back to my card game." He leaned forward as if to rise.

"Dad, listen to me," Kat implored, her voice shaking. "See, what I'm trying to say is that I almost died—"

Jake scratched the side of his unshaven face.

"That's right," Kat said. "Twice, in fact. Jodi here saved my life. Um, the first time she gave me, like, one of her kidneys after an accident I had." She rushed to get the words out before he cut her off again.

Jake sneered.

"You know what? I don't give a sh—"

Jodi pulled the phone away from her ear. Her heart ached for Kat. *No wonder Kat didn't visit her dad*, Jodi thought. She covered the mouthpiece and said to Kat, "Maybe it would be better if I just let the two of you talk, you know, without me."

Kat shook her head and mouthed the word *No.*

Jodi took a deep breath and then placed the receiver against her ear.

Kat cleared her throat. "Don't you care, Daddy, that I almost died? I owe her my life."

He laughed. "See, I deal with death every day." He stuck the cigarette in his mouth. "When I sleep, when I'm in the shower, when I'm in the yard. Anywhere, anytime, someone might try to stick me. Why? Because they want my cigarettes—or maybe it's my dessert . . . You came to the wrong place if you're looking for sympathy. End of story."

Jodi wanted to shout, "That's a cop-out—this is your daughter we're talking about," but she bit her tongue.

"There's something else," Kat said.

Jodi knew what was coming and felt the air crackle with tension.

"Make it fast," Jake said. "I've got cockroaches to chase in my cell."

Kat exhaled. "It was, like, about two weeks ago. I was lying in the hospital, not knowing if I was gonna live or die. And, well, it's hard to explain." She fell silent for a second.

Jodi, not wanting to be too obvious, used her foot to give Kat a reassuring nudge.

"Well, I was thinking about my life and how I always felt like there was this giant-sized hole inside." Kat brought a hand to her chest, and then placed it back on her lap. "Anyway, when Jodi came to see me, we talked about how God is the only One who can give my life, like, purpose. And I wanted that so bad I could almost taste it."

Jake leaned his head to one side.

"What I'm trying to say is that I prayed with Jodi for Jesus to change me," Kat said. Her eyes started to well up with tears. "I guess I just wanted you to know that I'm different now . . . and it's been great." She smiled softly, her eyes welling up with tears.

Jake rolled his eyes. "Of all the stupid things. Man, are you seriously messed up, kid." He took a drag.

"Actually, Dad, for the first time I feel like things fit together," Kat said. "Um, I guess I wanted to also say that I . . . I, like, forgive you for all the . . . stuff . . . you know, from before . . ." A lone tear rolled down her cheek.

Jodi reached over and squeezed Kat's arm.

". . . and, well, I'm praying for you, Dad, every day."

Jake stubbed out his cigarette in the ashtray. "Well, isn't that just dandy. The way I see it, you're still sick—in the head. And another thing, I'll tell you what you can do with your stupid Jesus guilt trip—"

Jodi couldn't contain herself any longer. She blurted, "Mr. Koffman, with all due respect, it seems you could use a healthy dose of fiber in your diet." *Where did that come from?* she thought.

Jake snapped his head around.

"What did you say?"

Jodi felt her skin crawl and her face flush, but the debater in her wouldn't back down. She held the phone tightly, her palm moist with sweat. "See, as I listen to the way you talk to Kat, I can't figure out what kind of *man* would be so cruel to his own daughter."

Neither spoke, their eyes locked together.

Jodi worked to control her breathing. "I don't pretend to know you, sir. And I don't know why you have so much hate bottled up inside. I do know Kat's changed, and—" Jodi said, stealing a look at Kat.

"Why don't you just shut up?"

Jodi ignored him. "Whether you care to admit it, she must really love you to put up with the heartless way you treat her."

"Shut up! Who do you think you are to lecture me?"

Jodi could see the hostility flare up in Jake's eyes. For an instant, she thought he would reach through the glass and choke her.

He pointed a long finger at Jodi. "Don't you come back here—ever." With that, Jake stood abruptly, still holding the receiver. He hunched down, his face so close to the window, steam from his breathing appeared on the glass.

"Kat, I don't care if I *never* see you again. Got it? Now get out of my face."

The sofa at Heather's house was one of the stiffest pieces of furniture Jodi could remember sitting on. She decided it was one of those looks-awesome-in-a-magazine-but-isn't-practical-for-actual-use accessories typically found in an upscale furniture store. Kat sat on Jodi's left, constantly shifting in place. *She's probably thinking about her dad*, Jodi thought.

Aside from Kat's initial apology for her dad's attitude and Jodi's affirmation of the way Kat had handled him, neither had said much during the forty-minute ride back from the prison to Jodi's house earlier that afternoon. They changed into their evening dresses with minimal conversation, too. Even now, Jodi wanted Kat to have all the space she needed to clear her mind. Jodi knew Kat would talk when she was ready.

"Any sign of the limo?" Kat asked.

Jodi looked out the oversized bay window to her right. It provided a sweeping view of Heather's manicured front yard and driveway. "Nope. Not yet," Jodi said. She offered a smile. "I imagine it'll be hard to miss."

The ticking of the grandfather clock filled the silence that followed. *She looks so much like her dad*, Jodi thought. *Same eyes. Same defined neck.*

"You know something?" Kat broke the stillness.

"What's that?"

"I've been thinking about my dad . . . you know, about today at the jail—"

"Kat, can I say something first?" Jodi asked.

Kat nodded. "Sure thing."

"Let me just say you were so, like, amazing," Jodi said.

"Me?" Kat's eyes widened.

"For real. I was so proud of you, Kat. I'm not sure I'd have been that gracious if he were my father."

Kat looked down at the coffee table. "Yeah, well, what I was about to say is that my dad is in more than one prison."

"What do you mean?"

"Of course, it sucks that anyone has to be in jail—although my dad deserves it," Kat said. She folded her hands in her lap; her eyes drifted to some faraway place. "But I've been thinking . . . The truth is, his heart is, like, locked up to the things of God. That's the real prison he's got to get out of—and he doesn't even know it."

Jodi placed a hand on Kat's shoulder.

"And," Kat continued, "he's shut me out so I can't help him find the way. You saw how mad he got when I talked about God, right? So what can *I* do?"

"*We* can pray for him together," Jodi said. "And then—"

"*Jodi!*" Heather shouted down the stairs. "John's gonna be here, like, any second and I'm not even ready!"

"Hold that thought," Jodi said to Kat, and then raced to the bottom of the staircase. "Whatcha need?" Jodi called back.

"Nothing, really," Heather said, leaning over the railing. "Just my stockings, my shoes, my purse, my cell phone—"

"Chill out, girl. Your purse is down here with your cell and that e-mail gadget thingy," Jodi said. "Want me to bring 'em up?"

"No, leave them there. And, like, if John comes to the door, just stall him for me, okay? But don't say anything."

Jodi figured Heather was referring to her last-minute decision not to go with John, a decision she had shared with Jodi and Kat an hour ago.

"As you wish." Jodi curtsied as if receiving orders from the queen of England. Right on cue, the grandfather clock chimed once, signifying the bottom of the hour.

"Would you get a look at this?" Kat said, followed by a piercing whistle. "It's gotta be the longest limo I've ever seen."

Jodi spun around for a look. She stood on her toes to peer out the beveled-glass window on the front door. *Kat's right*, Jodi thought. The sleek, thirty-six-foot white limousine filled the street. Although she didn't know much about cars, she couldn't help but recognize this one; a stretch Mercedes-Benz. Six vanity lights, mounted on the left and right sides of each black-tinted window, added to the air of opulence.

"John's here!" Kat yelped so loudly there was no need for Jodi to relay the message to Heather upstairs.

"Oh my gosh . . . oh my gosh . . ." Heather caught up her gown and scampered to the nearest window on the second floor.

"Yeah, and his limo is, like, the length of the whole street," Kat said. "I told you he was loaded!"

Jodi walked back to the stairs. "Heather," Jodi called in the calmest voice she could muster. "You sure you don't want my dad to do the talking?" She placed a hand on the banister.

Heather reappeared at the top of the steps. "No, I really think I need to be the one who tells John, you know? I mean, I got myself into this, so I should at least get myself out of it, right?" Heather played with one of her blond curls. "Gosh, he'll probably look at me like I've got ten heads when I tell him."

"You'll be fine," Jodi said. She didn't want to appear too excited that Heather had decided not to go with John. "Um, my dad's sitting in our car in case you need him. Better hurry, girl."

"Just give me a second," Heather said. "I'll be right down."

Jodi figured even though Heather wasn't going to the prom with him, she still wanted to at least make a good impression.

"Hey, the chauffeur dude just opened the rear door," Kat continued with her play-by-play. "Now he's walking up the sidewalk."

"John is?" Jodi asked.

"No, the chauffeur."

"Kat, stop staring out the window," Jodi scolded. "You don't have to be so obvious."

Kat joined Jodi in the hall. "Now who's uptight?"

Ten seconds later, the doorbell rang. Jodi reached for the doorknob and pulled it open. "Hi. Can I help you?" She glanced at the brass name-tag pinned to his jacket. It read: E. Smith.

"Good evening," the chauffeur said smoothly. Jodi noticed he was dressed in a charcoal-gray suit, complemented by an off-black shirt and silk tie. The red-tinted glasses seemed a little out of place, but there was no accounting for taste, she thought. A thin wire traveled from an earpiece to a point where the wire disappeared beneath his collar. Jodi guessed it was a hands-free cell phone, probably required of public transportation personnel as mandated by some new law.

He presented a business card with his gloved hand. "Would this be the residence of a Miss Heather Barnes?"

Jodi took the card. "It is," she said. She stood just two feet from the chauffeur, and yet, for some unknown reason, Jodi felt a degree of uneasiness stir within her. *What's up with that?* she thought. True, the man's accent sounded just a little too forced, as if he were trying to sound sophisticated. But, she decided, that was just part of the shtick.

"Mr. John Knox requests the honor of her presence," the chauffeur said, interrupting her thoughts with the same contrived intonation.

"Uh, Mr. Smith," Jodi said with a quick look at his name badge, "she'll be here in a minute." She managed a smile. As she waited for Heather, Jodi reviewed the business card with care as if it possessed some secret. Her eyes were drawn to the elegant scripting: *Leisure-Time Limousines.* She noted a Philadelphia address and phone number were printed across the bottom just below the slogan "For a Night to Remember." *It sure will be*, Jodi thought as she imagined Heather telling John to leave in his big limo—alone.

"Will you and your friend be joining us?" Mr. Smith asked with a nod in Kat's direction. "As you can see, we have plenty of room."

There's that feeling again, Jodi thought. Try as she might, she couldn't figure out what was fueling her anxiety. Maybe the sensation had something to do with her anticipation of John's reaction to Heather's last-minute rejection. Was that it? Then again, maybe Heather would discover John was a real hot guy, change her mind, and go with him to the dance after all.

"Actually, no. We have other plans . . . thank you very much," Kat said. She took the business card from Jodi and glanced at it.

Heather appeared behind Jodi. "I'm ready. Do I look okay?" She adjusted the shoulder strap of her purse.

"Whoa," Kat exclaimed. She placed the business card next to an arrangement of dried flowers on a table by the front door. "Talk about a knockout . . . you look like a million bucks!"

"Yeah, Heather," Jodi said with an approving nod. "You look perfect. And I love that dress on you. But how do you feel?"

Heather stepped forward and then out the front door. She looked back at Jodi and Kat. "Only, like, a train wreck."

The chauffeur checked his watch. "If you're ready, then, we better be going." He turned and then walked toward the limousine. Jodi watched as he left, his gait hindered by a slight limp.

Kat nudged Heather. "Hey, I thought you weren't—"

"Shh," Heather said. "I'll handle this. But you guys come with me to the car, okay?"

"Sure, go for it."

Jodi tagged along at Heather's side, wondering how Heather would bring up the subject. Jodi remembered her dad's suggestion that they do all the talking outside the car rather than getting in. Why risk being swept away by some stranger? Now, if Heather would only remember that bit of advice, too, she thought.

The limousine appeared to grow as they approached it, and just steps away, Jodi heard the soft hum of the engine idling. The thin black antenna mounted to the rear windshield added to the impression that important people were aboard. The chauffeur took his position by the rear side door, his gloved hands folded in front of him.

About five feet away, Heather said, "Gosh, I can't believe he's here." She flashed a nervous smile, crossed her fingers and then mouthed the words to Jodi and Kat, *Wish me well.*

Heather, holding her purse in her left hand, rested her right hand on top of the roof, nodded to the chauffeur, and then began to step inside.

"Oh my *gosh!*" Heather shrieked, her eyes as wide as saucers. "There must be some mistake."

Heather pushed herself away from the limo as if, by touching the vehicle, she had been shocked by a bolt of lightning. In her haste, she dropped her purse on the limousine floor. She staggered backward three steps and almost tripped over the curb. Jodi's arms shot out to steady her friend. What happened? What startled Heather? Was John a freak after all?

"What's wrong?" Jodi asked, unable to see inside the limo.

Heather brought a hand to her mouth, her face as pale as the moon. "I . . . don't believe it—"

Jodi looked over Heather's shoulder in time to see a burly figure in a tuxedo emerge. As he rose to his full height, Jodi gasped and blinked in disbelief. "What on earth?" she said under her breath. She felt the blood rush to her face. She had to suppress a yell of her own.

Jodi had been worried "John Knox" wasn't really the person he said he was. And now, face-to-face with him, she saw this guy didn't look anything like the guy in the photos. She was too stunned to do anything, although she felt the urge to punch him in the gut for deceiving Heather.

"Where's John?"

Follow me on this, people," Agent Nick Steele said. He straddled a stool in the FBI situation room, fingers wrapped around his suspenders. His eyes surveyed the faces of the six agents on his team. "The evidence we have leads me to believe we've got twenty-four hours—probably less—before this psycho kills again."

Dwayne raised a finger. "How do you figure?"

"Two things," Nick said. "First, his Web site promises a live feed sometime tonight, right?" Nick pointed at Frank and Steve.

"Affirmative," Frank said. "The perp bills it as a special event—get this—for an added charge."

"Ain't commercialism grand," Dwayne said, shaking his head.

"Given his track record," Nick continued, "he's planning to abduct a victim and then subject him or her to some intense fear stimuli. It's entirely possible he's already kidnapped his prey. We assume, but don't know for certain, that he kills his victims when he's finished with them. Second, the name of the promised broadcast is—" Nick snapped his fingers at his side. "Help me out here."

"Sir," Steve said, "he's calling it 'The Last Dance.'"

Nick nodded. He placed an unlit cigar in his mouth. "Think, men. What comes to mind—aside from the old Donna Summer tune?"

"The club scene," Tom said after a moment. "Gosh, there's probably several hundred clubs in Philly alone."

Nick shook his head side to side. "I'd rule them out."

"Because?" Dwayne asked.

"The people who go to those lizard lounges are older. Remember, you have to be twenty-one to get in." Nick cracked his knuckles. "And, for the most part, Billy's Web site features the faces of teenagers."

"Then maybe some kind of high-school graduation party?" Frank said.

Nick folded his arms. "Could be."

"What about a prom?" Hank asked.

"That's good. That's very good," Nick said. "Dwayne—"

"Sir?"

"We're pretty much past the prom season, so it should be easy to narrow down his potential targets. Start working the phones."

Dwayne took a deep breath. "Man, we're still talking about a few hundred schools in the Delaware Valley."

"What? Did you plan on sleeping tonight?" Nick turned to face Frank. "Can you tell us anything more about the location of his MegaFear.com Web server?"

"Yeah, and it's a problem," Frank said, leaning forward. "I've traced it to Southeast Asia. Somewhere in Bangkok, as a matter of fact."

Gene smiled. "Great, then let's shut this loser down—"

"Sorry, boys," Nick said. "Wish it were that easy. But the FBI can't waltz into the heart of Thailand and pull the plug. At least not without the cooperation of their government. That'll take more time than we have." Nick scratched the back of his head. "Besides, shutting down the Web site doesn't prevent the imminent threat."

With the exception of a buzz from the overhead fluorescent lighting, the room fell silent.

"Uh, sir," Tom said. "I may have at least something."

"Shoot."

"I checked around the dealerships," Tom said. "The ones across from the junkyard—like you asked."

"And—"

"Although the salesman couldn't remember the exact time, this morning a guy matching the perp's photo purchased a vehicle using the name 'Elvis Smith.'"

"What else?" Nick asked.

"Well, sir, he said three things bothered him." Tom consulted his notepad. "One, Elvis paid twenty thousand–plus in cash for an alpine-green XTERRA. Pulled the bills right out of a duffel bag. Two, he refused to provide a valid driver's license until the manager explained there was no way they'd make a sale without one."

"The third reason?"

"Oh, right," Tom said. "He claimed Elvis kept looking over his shoulder toward the street. Said he wore red-tinted glasses and didn't make any small talk. The guy was all business. Said Elvis kept telling him to hurry up. Made him nervous just being around the guy."

Nick stood up, cigar in mouth, and then placed his hands on his hips. "Plates?"

Tom shook his head. "No, sir. Just the usual temporary cardboard tag they tape to the rear window until the plates arrive by mail."

Nick lit his cigar. "I'll tell you what, men. Let's put out an APB with the description of Billy Bender, a.k.a. Elvis Smith, and his dark-green XTERRA to all police stations in the Delaware Valley. Pronto."

CHAPTER 20 ✦ FRIDAY, 5:36 P.M.

Stan? Stan Taylor," Jodi gasped.

"Surprise!" Stan said, his hands outstretched, his face morphed into an ear-to-ear grin.

"But, I don't get it. Where's John?" Heather asked.

"You're looking at him."

Heather folded her arms, flustered. She turned her back to Stan, trying to catch her breath. Her eyelids fluttered as they worked to keep her eyes from bulging almost out of her head.

Jodi looked over Heather's shoulder to shoot Stan a sharp look. She knew Stan "da Man" was more than their school's star defensive lineman. He was a seasoned practical jokester. At the moment, Jodi wanted to slam his 250-pound frame with the force of an offensive lineman back into the limousine.

Even so, she couldn't help but notice how Stan's black tuxedo draped his six-foot-four-inch frame perfectly. From the silken stripe, trimming the edge of his trousers the length of his leg, to the cummerbund around his narrow waist, Stan appeared flawless. *If only he had a clue*, Jodi thought.

"Hey, what gives?" Stan said. He raised his hands defensively. "Aren't we going to the prom, Heather?"

"Stan, like, c'mon," Kat said, taking several steps toward him. "Can't you see she was expecting somebody else?"

"I know that." Stan took a step forward. "If you'll just give me a chance, I'll explain—," Stan started to say, and then stopped. He turned around, reached into the limo, retrieved two dozen long-stemmed red roses, and then walked to Heather's side. "Here. I bought these for you, Heather."

Heather, who looked like a lost puppy, didn't immediately accept the flowers. By the look on her face, Jodi guessed Heather must be torn between the excitement of going with Stan to the prom and the disappointment that John, whom she had been expecting, didn't materialize.

"You want us to smack him for you?" Kat said, and then turned to face Stan. "Guys are so brain-dead. What's the big idea, huh?"

"Hold on a second," Heather said. "I'm . . . I'm just a little more than confused here—I mean, like, how can he be John?"

Jodi's dad, who had been waiting in his car, walked up to the group. "Is everything okay?"

"Well, yes and no," Jodi answered. "Uh, this is Stan, from school. He plays football." *Yeah, and he's just fumbled big time,* Jodi thought, but didn't say it.

"I'm Jodi's dad," Jack said, shaking Stan's hand. "Pleased to meet you."

"Likewise, sir."

"So where's John?" Jack asked. He looked at the limousine.

"We haven't gotten that far, Dad," Jodi said. "But don't worry, we'll work things out."

"Did John get sick and cancel or something?" Jack asked.

"Dad, it's okay, really." Jodi cleared her throat. "Hint, *hint.*"

Jack smiled. "Well, I can see I'm not needed. I guess I'll head on home. You guys have a nice evening."

"Oh . . . thanks for being here, Mr. Adams," Heather said.

"No problem. Glad to help." He headed back to his car.

Jodi called after him. "We'll talk later, Dad."

The group fell into an awkward silence as Mr. Adams drove away. The chauffeur raised a finger. "If I may interject, we'll be late for the pictures if a decision isn't made soon. And I have another pickup to make in forty-five minutes so we'll need to get going sooner than later."

"Can you give us a second?" Kat said.

The chauffeur nodded. "Certainly."

"Stan, what kind of sick joke is this?" Kat demanded, placing her hands on her hips.

"Wow—what's with the frontal attack?" Stan said, still holding the flowers. "You guys have gone psycho on me. All I was trying to do—"

Jodi interrupted. "Hold on, Stan," She reached for Heather's arm and gave it a squeeze. "Heather, do you want to go with Stan or us?"

"I . . . I'm not sure. I mean, of course I'd like to go with Stan. But, look at me," Heather said, touching her face. "My makeup's probably a total mess now."

"How about this," Jodi suggested. "Why don't you freshen up inside the house with Kat. That'll give you, like, a chance to clear your head and think about what you want to do tonight, okay?"

"Do you mind?" Heather asked Stan.

"Go ahead. Be my guest," he said. "I'll just put these in the limo for you." He spun around and stepped into the limousine with the flowers.

"Thanks, Jodi," Heather said with a faint smile. "I'll be just a minute. Come on, Kat," she said, tugging at her arm.

Jodi took several steps toward the house, then said, "Better hurry up." They disappeared down the sidewalk and into the house. Jodi, standing alone on the sidewalk, was bothered. For the life of her she couldn't figure out what Stan was up to by pretending to be John, and she didn't want to wait until after the prom to find out the juicy details from Heather.

There was one way to get to the bottom of the mystery. She walked to the limousine and then smiled at the chauffeur. "We need to talk," Jodi said, pointing toward Stan.

"Of course."

Jodi, careful not to agitate the bruised rib on her right side, slipped inside. Once seated, the chauffeur shut the door behind her. The thick, soundproof door closed with a soft click. For a split second, Jodi wondered why the chauffeur had shut the door, but figured it was a chauffeur's job to provide guests with some measure of privacy. Having never been inside a limo, Jodi was immediately distracted by her luxurious surroundings.

The air inside the spacious, padded compartment smelled of fresh, expensive gray leather. As her eyes adjusted to the muted, indirect interior lighting that lined the ceiling, she noticed a television set, outfitted with both a video and DVD player, mounted on the right side wall. The entertainment center was encased in a rich walnut trim.

Adjacent to the TV, a small refrigerator purred. Above it, a row of glasses and soft drinks awaited their turn. Immediately overhead she saw a console with a CD player and radio. The hushed sounds of classical music floated through the passenger compartment.

A long, comfortable seat stretched the length of the limo under the windows on the left side opposite the beverage bar. A cell phone occupied a space next to the armrest on Stan's door. Twenty feet in the distance, through a clear window separating them from the driver, she saw the Mercedes-Benz hood ornament perched on the top edge of the chrome grille. She sank down in the rear seat next to Stan.

Nice. Very nice. She could get used to this.

She was about to tell Stan off when she felt something at her feet. She leaned forward and saw Heather's purse. *Must have dropped it earlier*, Jodi thought. She picked it up and placed it on her lap. She'd give it to Heather as soon as she came out of the house.

"Well, looky here," Stan said, breaking the silence. "You wanna cruise the neighborhood?"

"Listen, big guy," Jodi began, still loaded for bear. "You didn't answer my question. What's up with all this John stuff?"

"What do you mean?" Stan offered a sheepish grin.

"Don't mess with me, Stan," Jodi said stiffly. "We don't have much time, and I'd like to—"

"Kiss me?" Stan puckered his lips.

Jodi raked her fingers through her hair. "Charming. Come to think of it, I'd rather kiss a frog."

"Aw, come on, Jodi. Lighten up. What do you want from me?"

"Try the truth."

Stan appeared wounded. "I already told you."

"You? You're John? I don't get it." Jodi's forehead scrunched into one long crease.

Stan nodded. "Yup. I be he. Or is it, he be me?"

"Cut it out," Jodi said. "What do you mean?"

"Just call me JesusFreakster2."

Jodi started to say something, and then stopped. *That's the screen name John Knox used*, she thought. But that was simply impossible to believe. "What in the world—"

"Gosh, give me a chance to explain." Stan scratched his chin. "See, all my life I've had to live up to this reputation of being, like, a ladies' man," he said, his tone more serious than Jodi had heard before. "And when I act that way—as I did with you a minute ago—that's how people expect me to act."

"Well, duh."

"Exactly. Hey, it's my own fault, I'll admit that. Being a jock and all, it kinda goes with the territory," Stan said. "Anyway, as you know, I used to go through girls, like, uh, . . . like—"

"Water?"

"Yeah. Can you blame me? I mean, with all these cheerleaders coming on to me . . . it's fun for a while, sure. But honestly? There's, like, more to me than what people see on the football field, you know?" He looked down at the roses on his lap.

"What's this got to do with Heather?"

"You mean, why I pretended to be John on-line with Heather?"

"Uh-huh," Jodi said, leaning her head to one side. She wasn't sure whether Stan was telling the truth or this was part of some big joke.

"Well, after spring break, I saw that you and Heather had something that was . . . that seemed real, you know?" Stan said. "And, I don't know . . . for the first time I wanted to be respectful of a girl—of Heather. Believe me, I didn't want to mess this up. Sounds corny, but I wanted to be liked for the person I am . . . or, at least, the person I'd like to be—"

Jodi was surprised at this side of Stan. "Well, nothing's wrong with that. But, why pretend to be—"

"John? Call it my fallback position."

"Your what?"

"My backup game plan. You know how I asked her to go with me, but she turned me down, right?"

Jodi nodded.

"So I figured this would be a way to get her to go with me anyway. Besides, when I was John, it was easier to be, like, real, you know? Talking with her on-line all the time, we got really close."

"Wrong-O, Stan. The whole thing was one big lie."

"That's not true, and it's not fair. Not everything was made up," he said, searching her eyes. "Okay, so the Christian stuff was made up—because it was important to her. But the other stuff we talked about . . . I really meant it."

Jodi flipped her hair over her shoulder. "Can't you see how you've confused things? She really cared for John, and John doesn't exist."

"I—

"No, listen to me," Jodi said, putting a hand on his arm. "Do you have any idea what she's been through? All this time we were worried John could be, I don't know, an ax murderer or something sick. And you know what?"

He raised an eyebrow. "What?"

"Heather was gonna tell John to get lost tonight—and then you stepped out of the limo. See?" Jodi put one hand on the seat between them. "That's why she's so confused. Didn't you think of that when you started this whole make-believe thing?"

Stan shrugged. "I guess . . . I guess I wasn't thinking that day."

"And you weren't honest with her," Jodi said, and then turned away.

She gazed out the window. It took a long moment for a new sensation to register.

"Stan, why are we moving?" she asked, watching the trees go by.

"We are? Gosh, maybe the driver's confused," Stan said with a nervous laugh. "Maybe he thinks you're going with me."

Jodi spun her head around. Her face felt suddenly warm. "I'm so sure. Heather's gonna come out of the house and we'll be gone. Then we'll both be in big trouble."

They laughed.

"So," Jodi said, "how do we tell him he's, like, made a mistake?"

"I think there's a button here that lets us talk to him." Stan reached up to an illuminated panel above their heads. He pushed one marked "Call Driver."

"Sir? Can you hear us?" Stan said in the direction of a small, built-in microphone by the switch. "Hell-o? Mr. Smith?"

No answer. Instead, a solid, mirrored panel, outfitted with fiberoptic twinkling lights and a Mercedes-Benz logo, rose between them and the front of the limousine. Once locked in place, the privacy barrier blocked their view of the driver.

"Stan," Jodi said, "what's going on?"

Okay, I'm ready. Let's go," Heather said, tossing her hairbrush into the bathroom drawer. She snapped off the light and then started down the stairs. "Oh, hey," she called over her shoulder. "Have you seen my purse?"

Kat followed in Heather's wake. "Didn't you have it with you, like, outside?"

Heather stopped at the bottom of the staircase. "You know, you're right. Come to think of it, I must have dropped it in the limo. At least that's the last time I remember holding it."

Kat walked past her and then looked out the front door. "Um, I hate to say it, Heather. But we've got a big problem."

"Let me guess. Stan and Jodi are fighting, right?" Heather came to Kat's side and then looked toward the street. She covered her mouth with a hand. "Oh my gosh! Where's the limo?"

"Beats me," Kat said. She opened the door and dashed for the sidewalk as fast as her dress would allow. Heather caught up with her at the curb.

"Did Jodi say anything about going anywhere?"

"No," Heather said, looking in both directions. She folded her arms together. "This is weird. I mean, *really* weird."

"Maybe they're just, I don't know, cruising around the block, checking out the ride," Kat offered. She stepped into the middle of the street for a better view.

Heather checked her watch and then shook her head. "Yeah, but we're gonna be late. This really bugs me. Stan knew we didn't have much time."

Kat returned to Heather's side. "Well, if your purse is in the car, why don't we, like, call them on your cell phone and tell them to get their butts back here."

Heather cracked a smile. "You know, that's a great idea."

Twenty seconds later, Heather and Kat were back in the house, hovering around the phone in the study. Heather picked up the handset and then dialed the cell. She pressed the phone to her ear. "Hi, it's Heather. Leave me a cool message and I'll get back to you—"

"Rats!" Heather said, returning the handset to its cradle. "The phone must be turned off." She blew a puff of air toward her bangs. "This is just not turning out to be my night."

Kat looked down. "Oh, I just remembered—the driver dude gave us his card. We could call the company and maybe they, like, could radio the limo or something."

Heather smiled. "Kat, you're amazing. Where's it at?"

"I put it over there . . . on the hall table," Kat said, moving into the hallway. She found the business card and then picked it up. "See?"

"Cool beans." Heather took the card from Kat and then hastily dialed the number. It was answered on the first ring. Heather cleared her throat. "Yes, um, I'm calling about a limousine for tonight . . . Well, no, I don't need to reserve one." Heather leaned against her father's desk as she spoke. "Actually, I'm calling because the limousine already came and left without me . . . My name? Heather Barnes."

Kat looked out the window. "Still nothing," she reported.

Heather switched the phone to her left ear. "Well, it was reserved by, um, Stan Taylor." She tapped her fingers on the desk, her nerves getting the better of her. "I'm gonna kill him if this is some kind of joke," Heather said to Kat under her breath.

"What do you mean there's no record of him?" Heather covered the receiver with her right hand. "Get this. They claim he never ordered one."

Kat turned around. "Oh, yeah, try John Knox," she said.

Heather nodded. "How about a John Knox? It could be under his name . . ." Heather twirled the phone cord around her finger. "No?"

Heather stiffened. "Ma'am, I know you're busy, but listen. A long, white limo—"

Kat whispered, "A Mercedes."

"Yeah," Heather said with a nod toward Kat. "It was a Mercedes-Benz, and it was sitting outside my house, like, ten minutes ago. I saw it myself—"

Kat stole another look at the street.

"No, this is not a prank," Heather said, frustrated. "The chauffeur handed me this card with your company's name on it . . ." Heather's voice rose several degrees. "Well, I'd sure like to speak with a supervisor . . . I see. Thanks anyway. Good-bye." She held the receiver for several seconds before hanging up.

"What gives?" Kat said.

Heather stared at Kat. "Do you remember the driver's name?"

"Isn't it on the card?"

"Nope—"

Kat closed her eyes for a moment. "It was . . . something-Smith. Maybe E. Smith—or B. Smith—but I couldn't swear for sure."

Heather picked up the card and aimed it at Kat as if it were evidence at a trial. "But are you sure this is the card the guy gave you?"

"Actually," Kat said, playing with an earring, "he gave it to Jodi, and then I took it from her. But, yeah. Why?"

Heather took two steps back and flopped down in her dad's leather chair. "The lady claims Leisure-Time Limousines doesn't own any white limos—or Mercedes."

The white limousine slithered like a snake into the flow of rush-hour traffic from the Willow Grove interchange. Billy, his gloved hands gripping the wheel, pointed the creature due west on the Pennsylvania Turnpike.

He lowered the visor to shield his eyes from the sun's angry glare as it began to sink into the horizon. Three lanes of bumper-to-bumper congestion littered the pavement as far as he could see. He checked his mirror, eased his way to the far left lane reserved for vehicles with three or more occupants, and then goosed the accelerator. The engine hummed as the beast sprang forward.

He checked his watch. Although the kids had delayed his departure, for the most part everything was going as planned. They were on their way and, he knew, would soon arrive at the prearranged destination in Valley Forge. Twenty minutes, tops.

As he drove, Billy recalled the months he usually spent on-line pretending to be someone he wasn't in order to win the confidence of some lonely teen. Inevitably, he'd suggest a face-to-face meeting, and so far, he'd never been turned down. The kids were all the same—stunned to learn they had placed their trust in somebody who didn't exist.

How gullible. How good for business.

He always took them for a ride, against their will. Not that they had a choice in the matter. And none would ever return home.

But this was different. It was the first time he had planned a totally random abduction of teens going to a prom. He figured that whoever got into the limo would star in his horror show. He knew after tonight he'd have to go back to the more tedious on-line seduction game. But for now, thanks to the cover the prom offered, he was enjoying an easy catch—and the prospects of big cash earnings from MegaFear.com.

Billy licked his lips. Jodi and Stan were about to make him and Jake a million dollars, minimum, and he could taste it.

Four lipstick-sized cameras, tucked in the four corners of the passenger compartment earlier that afternoon, were poised to capture the drama that was about to unfold. A miniaturized, omnidirectional microphone, also placed in the rear, would ensure a complete multimedia production. It was showtime. And it promised to be a long, intense night.

With a flick of a switch, Billy activated the cameras. A six-inch TV monitor, hastily mounted on the dash just above the radio, would display their every move. The screen was divided into four sections, one for each camera angle. The fearful reactions of Jodi and Stan would soon be transmitted around the world.

He guessed they'd try to open the doors.

He figured they'd try to open the windows.

He knew they'd be unable to escape.

And that was just the beginning.

For fun, he turned up the heat in the rear.

Billy wasn't expecting the call. In fact, he had told Jake he would be busy all night. And yet, his cell phone played the distinctive melody assigned to the pay phone in Jake's jail. Billy answered on the second ring.

"What?"

"Maybe I missed you," Jake said, the sarcasm dripping.

"Maybe I'm busy."

"Yeah, well, maybe I got a bad feeling," Jake said.

Billy looked in the rearview mirror. "You sure picked an awful time to get emotional," Billy chided. "Let me guess, they didn't serve cookies and milk at nap time—"

"Don't get stupid on me," Jake warned. He spat the words.

"Listen, man, I'm taking the kids on a field trip—"

"Where?"

"Does it matter?" Billy wasn't sure where this conversation was headed.

"Humor me. The TV's broken. Couple of guys smashed it during a Jerry Springer show. I could use some entertainment. Okay?"

Billy shook his head. "Washington Memorial Gardens, if it's all the same to you."

"I know the place," Jake said. "Two thousand–plus acres. Nice. You sure you're not being tagged?"

"Back off, Jake."

"No, *you* shut up and listen to *me*," Jake said. "See, I got me a mole inside the Feds. And you wanna know what?"

Billy didn't respond.

"They traced the Web server to Bangkok—although they can't touch it. They know something's going down this weekend. No specifics, just that it's happening. You listening to me?"

Billy felt a sudden surge of anger. He pounded the steering wheel. "What else haven't you told me?"

Jake coughed. "Listen, pal. I tell you what you need to know *when* I say you need to know it. That's how it works."

"I thought—"

"There you go again. Leave the thinkin' to me."

Billy, drumming the steering wheel with his gloved fingers, watched the white lines dividing the lanes on the road disappear under his bumper. "How'd you do it?"

"The mole? Easy." Jake laughed so hard, he started to cough. "Money is an amazing thing. Buys you just about anybody you want, see what I'm saying?"

"So what's the deal? You want me to abort tonight?" He looked at the video monitor and saw Stan reaching for the limo's built-in cell phone. "'Cause if you do, there'll be a few thousand disappointed subscribers—"

"Don't be stupid your whole life," Jake snapped. "Of course not. I'm saying, watch your back . . . cover your trail . . . and lay low after you're done."

"Yes, Mom," Billy said, his teeth clenched. "Now if you're done with the speech, I gotta go. The natives are getting restless, and I'm missing the show."

CHAPTER 23 ✦ FRIDAY, 5:55 P.M.

It's dead." Stan slammed down the car's built-in cell phone, then turned his head to the left.

Jodi studied the side of his face, his jaw grinding as he looked out the window. "Tell me, Stan," she said, placing a hand on his arm. "Is this a joke?"

Stan yanked himself free of her touch, tossed the roses on the floor, then looked her in the eyes. "I swear, Jodi, I have no idea what's going on."

She raised an eyebrow, still skeptical. "Well, whatever's going on, I'm sure we'll get out of this, no problem."

He turned his upper body toward her, extending his forefinger as he spoke. "All I know is that I ordered a limo to pick up me and then Heather. This guy shows up, gives me his card. Next thing I know, we're being taken who knows where. Plus, the phone doesn't work . . . the windows won't open . . . he's got the doors locked. Don't you get it? We're being kidnapped by some psycho chauffeur."

Jodi sighed. "And, I'm supposed to believe you . . . after what you did to me on the houseboat?" She folded her arms as the painful memory floated to the front of her mind.

Stan pounded his left hand against his door. "You still won't let that go, will you? I'm telling you, this ain't no gag." His voice cracked as he said the words.

Maybe Stan was telling the truth. He sure appeared genuinely worried, Jodi thought. Even his forehead was moist with sweat. Then again, he deceived Heather on-line, stringing her along for several weeks. The guy was a good actor. "I don't know," she said, looking down at Heather's purse in her lap.

"I'm serious. *I . . . don't . . . freakin' . . . know . . . what's up,*" Stan said, on the verge of tears. His chest heaving, he undid the top button of his shirt and then slumped back against the seat.

At the sight of Stan's face, filled with genuine fear, Jodi's heart jumped as if stabbed by a pitchfork. *What if Stan's right and we're being kidnapped?* she thought. She brought a hand to her mouth to contain a scream. Her face felt feverish. Her lungs struggled to pull in enough oxygen. She gasped. It was as if every nerve ending in her body suddenly went on red alert, reporting near-meltdown status.

For the first time, the long, narrow limousine felt more like a coffin than a car.

Jodi battled to keep her emotions in check in order to sort out the barrage of possibilities. Her dad wasn't rich. It wasn't like she possessed nuclear secrets or anything of significant value. Nor did Stan, at least as far as she knew. And yet she couldn't escape the question: *Why?*

Her thoughts were interrupted as Stan sat forward. He yanked off his tux jacket, and then, half standing, half crawling, started to make his way toward the front.

"What are you doing?"

He looked back over his shoulder. "I'm not gonna just sit here and let this jerk jag us around."

"Gosh, Stan, be careful—"

Stan, still crouching, balled his hand into a fist and banged against the mirrored privacy partition with the force of a battering ram. "Hey, you in there," Stan shouted. "Yeah, Mr. Clown Face . . . I'm talking to you. What's the big idea?"

With the third whack, the mirror cracked, cutting the edge of Stan's hand. He swore and then balanced himself on one knee. With all the force he could muster, he slammed the heel of his shoe into the barrier. Even though she sat a dozen feet away, Jodi covered her face as shards of the glass mirror crashed to the floor around Stan.

The thin plywood on which the mirror had been mounted was nearly busted through. Stan reared back for another kick. His foot was midair when the limousine driver slammed on the brakes, catapulting Stan into the partition. His leg hit first, then, helplessly, his shoulder and head followed. Under the force of the impact, Stan crumpled, falling into the collection of broken glass on the floor.

"STAN!" Jodi shouted, springing out of her seat. She was halfway up the center aisle when, unexpectedly, the limousine bolted forward. Stan, unable to balance, launched backward into Jodi's side with an unintended tackle. She yelped under Stan's massive frame as she fell to the carpet, her right side to the floor. Her fractured ribs throbbed.

Stan rose to his knees. "I'm gonna kill that moron," Stan said, picking himself up. "Here, take my hand." He extended his arm and then helped her to the backseat.

"You're bleeding," Jodi said, her breath coming in gasps, her rib cage burning as if on fire. She pulled her hair away from her face, then reached for and grabbed a handful of cocktail napkins and a bottle of water from the refreshment bar. With great effort, she twisted off the cap and then attempted to moisten the napkins. Her hands shook so violently, Jodi spilled half the bottle in her lap.

"Give me your hands," she said. Her heart rattled away as she worked. She wanted to wake up from this nightmare but didn't know how. If only she could think clearly.

"You *know* he did that on purpose," Stan snarled.

"You think he can see us?" Jodi asked, her forehead twisted into a maze of creases. She finished dabbing at his hands and then carefully wiped the side of his face.

"Ouch!"

"Sorry—"

"Here, let me do that," Stan said.

"Hold on, turn your head to the left," Jodi instructed. "I think I see a small piece of glass . . . don't move."

Stan complied. "I promise I'm gonna—"

"Shush." Jodi's eyes narrowed as she studied the wound. It wasn't deep, but the volume of blood complicated the task. "There." She held up the offending fragment, then pitched it as far forward as she could. It landed in the pile of shattered remains from the mirror.

It was then that the television blinked on. A dark silhouette of a man's face appeared. Jodi's heart suddenly worked overtime as she focused on the image filling the screen.

"What the—," Stan started to say.

"This is your chauffeur speaking," he said, his voice heavily affected. "My name is Elvis. I trust you're enjoying your—"

Stan bristled. "Why don't you stuff your head—"

"Shut up, guy." This time, the voice was sharp. "And don't try another stunt like the last one or the consequences will be . . . painful."

Stan scowled at him. "Come on, big man. Why don't you pull this thing over. I'll take you on right now."

Jodi watched in disbelief as the chauffeur produced a gun.

"*Stan* . . . shut up . . . Do what he says," Jodi said, her voice trembling.

"Smart lady," he said, lowering the gun. "In a few minutes, I'll be stopping the car. You'll both do exactly what you're told. The first person to step out of line gets shot, see? No warnings. Until then, enjoy a beverage. They're complimentary."

The TV went blank.

At first, Jodi was too stunned to move. Sixty seconds later, she managed to glance at Stan. The arteries on the side of his neck throbbed. She could only guess what was going through his mind. "*Jesus . . . Jesus.*" Jodi whispered a prayer.

"This nut case is gonna kill us," Stan said, removing his jacket. "You know that, don't you?"

A stream of hot tears began to roll down her face. She wiped at them with the back of her hand. "Now what?"

"You bring your cell phone?"

Jodi shook her head slowly. "No . . . but, wait." She looked around for Heather's purse as a new idea came to mind. She spotted it several feet in front of her on the floor. "Can you, like, grab that for me? My side's killing me."

Stan extended his leg, hooking the toe of his shoe in the strap, then dragged it within reach. He handed the thing to Jodi.

"I think Heather has a phone," she said, tearing into the purse. "Yes!"

Jodi turned it on. It chirped as it powered up. Jodi waited for the display to finish its opening sequence. She turned to Stan. "Gosh, any idea where we are?"

Stan looked out his window. Jodi did likewise. She had to squint to see through the dark window tint. The phone beeped, and Jodi stared in disbelief at the display. "Rats. Heather never keeps this thing charged," she said. "There isn't much battery left."

Her hands shook as she raced to dial her home number. Her mind was in overdrive trying to decide what to say. No telling how much time she'd have before the thing cut off. "Come on, come on." Jodi pressed the phone to her ear with both hands. She heard it connect.

It rang once.

Twice.

"Answer already—please!"

Her heart stopped when, on the third ring, the answering machine clicked on. She desperately needed to hear the reassuring sound of her dad's voice. He'd know what to do. He'd know who to call. *Where was he?*

Without warning, the speaker system in the back of the limousine erupted with the diatribe of some gangsta rapper who boasted of bustin' heads and killin' cops. His rap thundered, bass heavy, through the system at full volume. Jodi shrieked, her eardrums on the verge of bursting. "Turn that thing off!"

"It's not me," Stan shouted back, trying to shut off the radio. "It's him . . . it's him!"

"I can't hear a thing!" Jodi cupped the mouthpiece with her hand. She yelled, "Dad, Mom, it's me. I don't know if you can hear me. Stan and I . . . we've been kidnapped . . . in that white limo . . . The driver thinks he's Elvis . . . and we're—"

"Hold on," Stan barked. "The Valley Forge exit—"

"We're on the turnpike . . . the Valley Forge exit . . ."

Three rapid beeps in her ear signaled the battery was drained. A second later, the connection died. Jodi swallowed hard, lowered the phone, and stared at the blank screen. Knowing she might never speak with her parents again, a stream of fresh tears formed at the corners of her eyes.

If only she had another second to say, "I love you guys."

She started to sob.

Rebecca Adams staggered in the front door like a pack mule bearing more than its share. Groceries stuffed into plastic bags stretched to their max hung from each arm. She called out, "Can you get the phone, hon?"

"I'll get it." Jack knew she hated missing even one call. He scrambled down from the attic, the rickety pull-down ladder wobbling with each step. He managed to answer on the third ring. "Hello? This is Jack."

"Mr. Adams? It's Heather Barnes. I'm so glad you're finally there."

"Oh, hey Heather." Jack checked his watch. "Actually, I've been home for at least twenty-five minutes. Been working in the attic. I must not have heard the phone. What's up? You girls find a nice spot for dinner?" He plucked a clump of pink attic insulation from his T-shirt, then tossed it in the trash can by the desk.

"Um, actually, that's why I'm calling," Heather said.

Jack couldn't miss the nervousness in her voice. "What's wrong, Heather?" Through the kitchen door, he watched his wife dump the bags on the floor and then sprint outside for more.

"I . . . I don't know exactly how to say this but, like, the limousine's gone . . . It left with Stan and Jodi . . . and it still hasn't come back." Heather choked up.

"Okay, take it easy, Heather." Jack reached for a pen and yellow writing tablet. "Did they say they were going to leave?"

"No."

"Well, when did this happen?"

"Maybe, a few minutes after you took off," Heather said. "See, Kat and I went into the house to, like, do some things. We left Stan and Jodi by the limo. When we came out, they were gone. And that's *so* not like her."

"I agree," Jack said, "But I'm sure there must be a simple answer." He instinctively attempted to organize the data. He remembered tuning into KYW news radio at 5:40 to catch the weather report as he drove away. He made a note of the time on the pad. "How long were you inside the house?"

"Um, not more than, say, five or ten minutes."

"So, sometime between 5:45 and 5:55 the limo left with Jodi and Stan. Any idea where they went?" he asked, but already guessed at the answer.

"I don't have a clue, and I'm really worried, Mr. Adams."

Although he, too, felt a growing uneasiness, he didn't want to further upset her. "I appreciate your concern, Heather," Jack said. "Is there anything else you can tell us?"

"Yeah. What's really weird is the limo company."

Jack switched the phone to his left ear. "Go on, I'm listening."

"Well, the chauffeur gave Jodi and Kat his business card. I've got it right here," Heather said. "Anyway, I called the number, and the company claims they didn't schedule a pickup or whatever at my house tonight."

"I see," Jack said, his palms getting sweaty. "Did you happen to get the driver's name?"

"Uh-huh," Heather said. "Kat thinks his nametag said something like E. Smith or maybe B. Smith—but she doesn't remember for sure."

"What about a description? I didn't get a good look at him from where I sat in my car."

"Sure. I'd say he was taller than Jodi, but shorter than Stan. I remember he had red-tinted glasses—kinda odd goggle-shaped things." Heather paused, then added, "His outfit was all black and, oh, yeah . . . he walked with a limp."

Jack carefully documented the details as she spoke. "Why don't you—"

"Excuse me," Heather said, interrupting. "I forgot the gloves. He wore black gloves. I remember noticing them when he, like, held the door open for me."

"Very good, Heather. Why don't you stay close to the phone and keep an eye out front just in case they come back."

"We will," Heather said. "I only wish I had the license number of the car, not like I ever thought—"

She no sooner spoke the words when a mental picture of the license plate steered back into Jack's mind. As a kid, he used to pass the time on long family trips picking out unusual license plates from passing cars, a peculiar habit he never let go of. "Odd you should mention that, Heather. I happened to notice it was 'Lv2Danc.'"

"You did? How awesome!"

"Look, I better run." He exchanged good-byes and then stared at the notepad, tapping the end of his pen on the desk.

Rebecca returned with several more bags. "Jack, you look worried. What is it?"

He looked up from his notes. "Come here, hon."

Rebecca came to his side.

"We don't know where Jodi is—"

"What are you saying?" She dropped the bags to the floor.

"Heather just called," Jack said, reaching for her hand. "For some reason, Jodi and Stan left in the limo and haven't returned. And, it's been half an hour."

She searched his eyes. "Well, there's got to be a good explanation. Did she call us?"

"Not that I know of," he said. "But I've been in the attic since I got home."

Rebecca hurried to the answering machine in the kitchen, Jack just steps behind. "There's a message," she said. She pushed the play button, then folded her arms. Jodi's voice, shouting over the jarring gangsta rap music, filled the room. Jack listened in silence. Rebecca embraced herself as if chilled.

When the message ended, Rebecca cupped her mouth. She gasped, "Oh, dear God." She pushed play again.

"I'm calling the police," Jack said. "Where's the phone book?" He scrambled around the kitchen like a caged animal, opening cabinet doors. "How come I can't ever find anything around here when I need it?"

Jodi's mom pulled the book from the top drawer by the dishwasher and handed it to him, too stunned to speak.

Jack snatched the phone off the wall with his left hand as he flipped through the blue pages with his right, searching for the local police department number.

"Jack, why don't you just call 911?"

He blinked. "You're right. What was I thinking?" He punched in 911 with enough force to bruise the numbers. It was answered almost immediately.

"Yes, ma'am, my daughter's been kidnapped, about a half-hour ago and . . . Excuse me? . . . Yes, please, I'll take that number . . . Could you repeat that? Thank you." He clicked off and then started to dial again.

"What happened?"

"Kidnappings are a federal crime," he said. He placed the phone to his ear. "I'm calling the FBI."

Agent Nick Steele stared out the window at the statue of William Penn. His half-smoked cigar sat neglected in the ashtray next to the phone on his desk. Although not a religious man, and certainly not a Quaker like Penn, Nick considered himself an honest man. Sure, he'd bend a few rules now and then. In his view, that's how things got done. And right now, in order to nail Billy Bender, he needed to stretch the truth.

Life was, after all, a series of trade-offs.

He reached for his secure phone line and started to dial.

"Nick," Dwayne said, barging into his private office.

Nick hung up.

"Sorry—I have something hot here." Dwayne held a piece of paper in his hand as if he were holding the winning Lotto numbers.

Nick just nodded.

"I spoke to a Jack Adams," Dwayne said. "Seems his daughter and another junior, Stan Taylor, from Fort Washington High School, were picked up in a white limousine—it's prom night."

He reached for the stub of his cigar and, with it, waved Dwayne on.

"The deal is, Jodi—that's Jack's girl," Dwayne said, slightly winded, "managed a panicked call from the limo claiming she'd been kidnapped."

"By who? The boy?"

"No. She said, 'The driver thinks he's Elvis—'"

Nick closed his eyes for a second, rubbed his temples and then looked at Dwayne. "Tell me where? When?"

"In Huntingdon Valley, maybe forty-five minutes ago." Dwayne handed him the paper. "Year, make, model—even the license of the limo—it's all there."

Nick scanned the page. "You trace the plate yet?"

"Yes, sir. It's owned by Premier Limousines," Dwayne said. "I called, and boy, is the owner hacked. He confirmed the limo and scheduled pickup were theirs. And, another thing. He said the driver was a new employee—his first night, actually."

"This employee—what name did he use?"

"Elvis Smith."

Nick stuck the cigar in his mouth, then folded his hands. He figured they could bust Billy for at least two counts of kidnapping—that is, if they could pinpoint him in time. This was the break he was looking for. Catch the bad guy with the goods. "Last known location of the limo?"

"The Turnpike, headed for the Valley Forge exit."

"That's it?" Nick frowned. "Valley Forge covers how many thousands of acres?"

Dwayne shrugged. "I understand your frustration, sir." He loosened his tie. "But, see, her phone went dead before she could say anything else."

Nick scratched the back of his neck. This new development only served to validate his decision. "Thanks for this. Now, if you'll excuse me, Dwayne. I need to make a call. Maybe get me some coffee—black. Okay?"

"Sure thing." He turned to leave. "What'll I say to the family?"

"Tell 'em we're on it—now pull the door on your way out."

For the better part of his career, Nick had been assigned to prosecute hard-core pornography. He quickly discovered most porn was produced by one of the five organized crime families in America, who also controlled the distribution. Under Presidents Ronald Reagan and the elder George Bush, Nick busted bad guys right and left, especially those engaged in child porn.

But when Bill Clinton became president, enforcement of obscenity laws ceased being a priority. Nick was peeved when his duties were reassigned to other domestic matters. It ticked him off the way porn merchants, using the Internet, transformed the nation into one sick peep show.

With George W. Bush's administration, fighting porn was again a genuine priority. One of Nick's first cases under the revamped "Innocent Images" program involved a scheme to sell child porn on the Internet. Although Nick had never met the man he was about to call, Nick was responsible for putting him behind bars, for twenty years.

Nick stared at his phone.

He knew he needed the help of this prisoner. He knew the prisoner was looking to broker a deal. Jake Koffman initiated the contact one week ago, offering to double-cross his partner in exchange for his freedom. Having spoken with Jake several times since then, Nick knew Jake would be willing to sell his mother's soul if it meant getting out of jail.

So far, Jake's information had proved accurate.

The tip on Elvis staying at the RV park.

The Web hosting in Bangkok.

The limousine abduction.

In return, Nick knew Jake expected an early release. But the thought of sending Jake back to the streets, where he would most likely return to his revolting child-porn trade, irked Nick. On the other hand, Nick wanted to prevent the imminent death of two kidnapped teens—not to mention future abductions for use on the MegaFear.com site.

Nick dialed the number. He would just figure some way to send Jake back to the pokey. He had to. Nick knew it was mealtime at the Trenton prison, and Jake would be sitting near the pay phone, expecting the call.

"Joe's Bar 'N' Grill," Jake said, answering on the second ring.

A real comedian, Nick thought. "I need a piece of information," Nick said without identifying himself.

"We got a deal, right?" Jake said.

Nick hesitated. "Remind me."

"Hey, don't go getting stupid with me," Jake said. "You said time served for good behavior. I'm feeding you gems here. I'm not about to take food stamps for what I'm givin' you."

"I said I'm still working on it. There was a small complication. Things aren't always that easy—"

"Whoa . . . what's this I'm hearing?"

Nick folded his hands behind his head. "I told you I'd take care of you. That's a promise."

"Yeah, I'd say you did a pretty good job takin' care of me already," Jake said, then coughed. "Got me twenty years in the slammer."

"Why don't you give me something to sweeten the pot," Nick said, grabbing at straws.

"That's the way you wanna play it? Fine." Jake paused. "Um, it's going down tonight."

"We already know that."

"Yeah, well, he's got two kids—"

Nick laughed. "Like I said, give me something that's not in yesterday's paper."

"Like what?"

"How about a location? It's a big world, pal." Nick rotated in his chair. His eyes drifted down to the traffic clogging Broad Street.

"I can do that. Hold on—"

Nick waited.

"I'm back," Jake said. "A guy almost swiped my dinner—"

"Get on with it, Jake, or start planning to eat that stuff for the next two decades."

"Listen, man, he's taking them to Valley Forge."

"This conversation is over, Jake." Nick gripped the phone. "You wanted your free pass out of jail, but you're giving me zip. Forget about it."

"Hey, why do you got to act like that, man?"

Nick clenched his teeth. "I don't have time to worry about your mystery meat, not when the lives of two kids are on the line. Now, are you gonna talk or not?"

"Do I get out of here now, or not?"

Nick shrugged. "Like I said—"

"Then I say, let 'em rot in hell. And another thing—"

Nick was immediately out of his chair, jabbing at the air with his finger. "Shut up and listen to me, Jake. If those kids die, I promise you'll be in for life."

"Yeah, right, like how?"

"I'll nail you as an accessory to a double murder."

Nick slammed down the phone.

CHAPTER 25 ✴ FRIDAY, 6:35 P.M.

The limousine bounded down Route 23 East, a little-traveled stretch of road five miles from the Pennsylvania Turnpike. Jodi had committed to memory every significant turn, road, and landmark since leaving the toll road. Such details could make all the difference if they were to escape. Not that she'd ever get the chance to use the information. As her mother always said, "You just never know."

In a general sense, Jodi was familiar with the area. She'd been to the King of Prussia mall several times before, usually around Christmas. A sprawling upscale collection of stores, it was located just off the Valley Forge interchange. But the combination of twisting, two-lane back roads started to blur together into a map of confusion.

Jodi's heart spiked as the limousine pulled through the entrance of the Washington Memorial Gardens. Why was he taking them to a cemetery? Were they hostages? Was he planning to torture them? She didn't have a clue, and for the life of her, she wished she could just blink, wake up, and find it was all a terrible dream.

She looked over at Stan. Aside from the dried blood, his face appeared pale—probably from the stress of not knowing what awaited them. As strong as he was, he seemed powerless to do anything. She wanted to know what he was thinking, but his body language suggested he was in no mood for talking. Besides, there was no point trying to talk above the wild music still blasting away at what remained of her eardrums.

She looked out her window. She'd been here once before, years ago. The cemetery, she recalled, was on the edge of Valley Forge National Park. Her ninth-grade history class, along with just about every other school in Philadelphia, toured this historic battleground where George

Washington camped during the Revolutionary War. Her mind was happily distracted by the memory.

As a kid, she thought it was cool to tour Washington's headquarters and check out the log cabins, see the cannons, even visit the gift shop, all of which peppered the lush, green rolling hills of the park. She loved the Patriots Tower and Washington Memorial National Carillon, a graystone structure, which they had just passed. She remembered the guide saying the bell tower housed fifty-eight tuned brass bells and a full-size replica of the Liberty Bell.

Liberty. How she longed to be free again.

The limousine skidded to an angry stop, jolting her into the present moment. Jodi held on to keep from pitching forward. Regaining her balance, she cupped her hand above her eyes and pressed her face to the window on her right.

As best she could tell with the shadows of tall trees shrouding her view, they were somewhere near the edge of the cemetery by a forest. Several of the grave markers were tall, towerlike, and pierced the evening sky. Most, she saw, were waist-high, thin, and made of gray granite streaked with weather stains. Others were just stubs, barely twelve inches tall. All appeared older than time itself.

The music stopped cold.

A deafening silence filled the car.

Moments later, she heard the trunk open, then slam with a thunk. Elvis appeared outside her door, holding a duffel bag and a lantern, its flame dancing in place.

Jodi's skin crawled as if covered by a million ants. Her chest was suddenly too tight to permit breathing. She turned to Stan, her throat dry as desert sand. "I . . . I'm really scared."

He reached over and clutched her hand, then leaned toward her window for a better look. "Can you see what the creep is doing?"

"Look's like he's putting some stuff on top of the car," she said, nervously hooking her hair over her right ear.

"You think your parents got the message?"

"Gosh, I sure hope so . . ."

Elvis yanked Jodi's door open. Instinctively, she shrank back as if confronted by an angry skunk.

Like an executioner, Elvis, now wearing a black ski mask, stood with his gun pointed at Jodi. "You—out of the car."

"*Stan!*"

"Do what he says," Stan said, his voice unsteady. "We'll think of something."

She slid out, legs first, clutching Heather's purse like a five-year-old holding her lunch box on the first day of school. She stepped onto the ground. Around the edges of her white sandals, she could feel the sharp, uncut grass graze against her skin, like needles.

"Turn around. Face the car." Elvis brandished his gun at Jodi as he spoke.

She complied, slipping the purse over her shoulder. As she turned, she scanned her surroundings. It dawned on her how isolated they were. No visitors were in sight. No signs of life anywhere. She heard a dog barking and figured it had to be a stray. There wasn't a house for miles.

She looked toward the cloudless heavens. The full moon, already positioned high in the sky, complemented the comforting glow of the setting sun in the horizon. She whispered, "Jesus . . . *please* . . . we need you."

"Now, you, big guy," Elvis said pointing at Stan. "Get out, face the trunk of the car. Put your hands behind your back. Try anything funny and I *will* shoot you—that I promise."

From the corner of her eye, she watched Stan ease out of the seat. He appeared defeated, shoulders slumped, head down. Even so, Jodi wouldn't put it past Stan to try to tackle this guy.

"Okay, girlfriend, take the duct tape," Elvis said, pointing toward the top of the roof above the door where Stan had exited. "Tie his hands together."

Jodi hesitated.

"DO IT!"

She reached for the tape and, suddenly lightheaded, dropped the roll to the ground. "Oh my gosh! Sorry. I—"

Elvis pulled the hammer back on his gun with a click. "Idiot! Pick it up—real slow like."

Jodi felt the blood rush to her face as she squatted down. She retrieved the tape, her hands shaking out of control, peeled back a six-inch section, then began to bind Stan's wrists together.

"Now," Elvis said, "tape his fat mouth shut."

Stan turned his head around and then spat at Elvis. "Nice. Get a girl to do your dirty work." For a second, Stan puffed out his chest like a street fighter looking for a brawl. "What kind of man are you?"

Jodi shrieked as Elvis aimed the gun, then fired two shots three inches from Stan's feet. Although the silencer muzzled the sound, the bullets plowed into the ground with distinctive thuds. Stan jumped, slamming against the side of the limousine.

Jodi, tears streaming down her face, helped Stan up. She tore off a section of tape and said just above a whisper, "I'm sorry to do this."

"Jodi, I swear I'll kill him," Stan said, his eyes narrowing.

She covered Stan's mouth as gently as possible with a four-inch piece.

"Now, little girly," Elvis said, "put that bag on his head."

Jodi felt her blood boil. "Please, don't make me do that—"

"Fine. Then I'll just duct-tape his eyes shut," Elvis said. "Is that what you want?"

Jodi reached for the bag.

"We have names, you know," Jodi said, surprising herself. She didn't mean to say anything more. She certainly didn't want to provoke the monster. The words just sort of came out. She placed the cloth bag over Stan's head.

"Names are unimportant in my line of work," Elvis said, his tone devoid of feeling. "Now, toss me your purse, missy."

She opened her mouth to explain it wasn't her purse, but changed her mind. He stood six feet away and Jodi was careful with her aim. She figured he was looking for another cell phone, mace, or pepper spray, since most girls didn't pack a knife or gun on a date.

He caught the purse by the strap, his firearm still directed at them.

"Let's see what other goodies are in here." He rifled through it, then, with a grunt, tossed it back at her.

"Now, listen to me good," Elvis said. "Take him by the arm and lead him down this path." He pointed to a narrow dirt trail leading toward the darkness of the woods. "I'll be ten steps behind you. I promise—if you run, scream, or draw attention to us, I'll put a bullet in the base of your neck. Got it?"

Jodi managed a nod. For a second, she worried the jackhammering of her heart was making too much noise. She slipped her hand through Stan's arm and started to walk. For the life of her, she couldn't imagine what Elvis wanted. If he was set on killing them, why not just do it now and get it over with? Why all the theatrics?

She struggled to make sense of her circumstances.

She was a captive.

Walking in dark shadows.

Through a cemetery.

With a gun pointed at her back.

Was it bad luck—or mere chance—that she happened to step into the limousine instead of Heather? Was it the luck of the draw? A lousy coincidence? Or, worse—was it God's will?

She looked skyward. *Is this your will, God?* If so, she couldn't imagine her death benefiting anyone.

A cool breeze drifted across her path as the words of Jesus came to mind: *My grace is sufficient for you, for my power is made perfect in weakness.*

A minute later, she heard Elvis bark, "Stop right there." He walked beyond her carrying his bag and the lantern. He stopped several steps in front of the door of an ancient mausoleum.

The flicker of the lantern cast an eerie light against the stone tomb. It resembled a small house, probably fifteen feet wide and as many feet deep. A set of two columns, positioned on both sides of the door, supported the porch roof. A round placard was mounted above the door at the apex of the roof. Two stone lions, one on either side of the steps, guarded the entrance.

Elvis dropped his bag and pulled the metal door outward with two hands. Picking up the bag, he stepped inside and then hung the lantern from a beam near the ceiling. He appeared to take something out of the bag and place it on the floor, but she couldn't tell for sure what it was.

Jodi squinted at her watch. With the sun receding, the night air turned chilly enough to produce goose bumps on her arms, although the situation unfolding in front of her was already doing a pretty good job of that.

Elvis stood just outside the door. "Take him inside."

Jodi stammered, "I . . . I don't understand, sir."

Elvis stared at her through his mask. "What's to understand?"

"Just, like . . . why? Why'd you pick on us?"

He rested a gloved hand on the head of the lion statue, then drummed his fingers. "Since you're not going anywhere, why not? I usually pick up kids from the Internet—eighteen kids have been dumb enough to meet me already, see." His fingers crawled over the head of the lion, sticking into the eye cavities. "You might say I had it down to an art form. But tonight was different. By posing as a limo driver, I didn't have to listen to your stupid problems and pretend to give a rat's butt." A wicked laugh escaped his mouth. "Besides, for a million bucks? Why not? Now, move."

Jodi's feet felt as if they were encased in cement. Try as she might, she couldn't budge.

Elvis stomped toward her, his eyes shooting daggers through the slits in the ski mask. He seized her by the arm, then dragged her into the death chamber. With a shove, she fell to the cold stone floor. On impact, her cracked ribs burned with pain. Seconds later, Stan crashed to the floor beside her.

Elvis appeared at the doorway. He sneered, "It's not the Taj Mahal, but at least you're going out in style."

CHAPTER 26 ✦ FRIDAY, 7:05 P.M.

Jodi stared in disbelief as Elvis closed the door, shutting out all contact with the world of the living. A moment later, as her surroundings blinked into view, a sense of finality settled in. No windows. No light, aside from the lantern with its meager supply of oil. No bathroom. And the air, musty, almost thick enough to choke on, stank like stagnant water.

This wasn't happening.

What she wouldn't give to break free.

She had her whole life ahead of her. Now she'd never see college, pursue a career, get married, or have kids. All her dreams stopped the minute she stepped into the limousine. A hollow fear sent her stomach into her throat as if she'd just stepped off a cliff.

Lying on her side, she coughed three times. The dust, thicker than the layer under her bed at home, chafed her lungs. She longed for a hot shower, but would settle for a garden hose. She propped herself up on one arm, her tears mingling with the dust, and cried, *"Oh, Jesus . . ."*

She felt as if she were headed for a complete breakdown. The taste of panic, like bile, churned in her stomach. In her mind's eye, she imagined seeing her name in the obituary column next to some eighty-year-old who'd lived a full life and died of natural causes. To die this young, and like this, just wasn't fair.

And yet, in the next inexplainable moment, story after story of God doing the impossible for those he loved flooded Jodi's mind. She remembered that God silenced the lions for Daniel in the lions' den . . . he parted the sea for the Israelites, when the Egyptians were in hot pursuit . . . Jesus calmed a storm at sea with just a word, when the disciples thought they were sure to die . . . and he raised Lazarus, who *had* died.

Even a grave was no match for God.

A peace she couldn't explain, like a warm comforter, suddenly wrapped around her. In spite of how things appeared, she sensed the presence of God. He hadn't abandoned her. Nor would he, of that she was sure.

Stan, kicking, struggled to upright himself, hands still bound, face still hooded. She put aside her thoughts, rose from the floor to a half crawl and, favoring her bad side, inched toward Stan. "Hold on . . . hold on. Let me help you." Her voice echoed against the thick, stone walls.

Stan stopped thrashing as she removed the hood. His eyes, wild with intensity, nose flaring, startled her. She reached to pull off the tape covering his mouth.

"Mmm—mm!!"

"What? I'm just gonna—"

"MMMM!!!" Stan shook his head violently, motioning to his hands.

"Okay, okay. Calm down." With some effort, Jodi freed his hands of their makeshift shackle. "There. Done." She fumbled for Heather's purse and then dragged it with her as she leaned against the side wall. She drew her legs to her chest.

Stan shook out his arms, scratched at his wrists like a rabid dog, then carefully peeled the tape from his mouth. He choked down a mouthful of air. "Just let me get my hands on that loser for one second—ONE SECOND."

He sprang to his feet, his tux covered in grime, then crashed his shoulder into the front door with a smack.

It didn't budge.

He rammed it again, harder. He swore. He massaged his shoulder, obviously bruised by the encounter. Angered, he reared back and like a bulldozer, plowed into it with both feet. He repeated the action several times, shouting, "*Let . . . us . . . out . . . of . . . here!*"

The door, sturdy as a bank vault, offered no movement.

With a flurry of fists, his hands blasted the door. His feet alternately kicked the base of the door. His energy spent, Stan flipped his middle finger at the door in a lewd jesture, then slumped to the floor next to Jodi, defeated. His chest heaved; a bead of sweat thickened on his dirty brow.

Stan's head wobbled toward Jodi. His face caked with dirt. "Now what?"

Jodi didn't immediately answer. She stared at the lantern's flickering flame; her thoughts drifted back to spring break. She, Stan, and six other classmates sat around a campfire. Was that really just a couple of months ago? Stan had told the group he had a part-time job last summer as a grave digger. The experience made him wonder if death was really the end.

Jodi blinked. She looked into his eyes. Maybe this whole ordeal wasn't about her. Maybe being trapped with Stan was some kind of divine appointment. *Was that it, God?* She brushed several strands of hair from her face.

Stan waved his hand in front of her face. "Hello . . . earth to Jodi."

"Sorry. I was just thinking . . . about stuff."

"Like, what?"

"About God—"

Stan folded his arms. "Yeah. Me too."

Jodi's right eyebrow shot up. "Really? Like, how?"

"No offense," Stan said, reaching up to rub his shoulder, "I can't understand how you Christian-types think God is so loving when he does stuff like this."

Jodi winced. "What?"

"Well, maybe you haven't noticed"—Stan swept his hand through the air—"but there's no kitchen. No water. No door handle on the inside of the door, not that Mr. Cadaver would ever go for a stroll."

"Nice, Stan."

"And, you know what? I dug graves last summer—"

"I know—"

"Yeah, well, let me tell you a thing or two about our Corpse Hotel," Stan said, crossing his legs Indian style. "Did you know these vaults are almost airtight?"

"For real?" Jodi felt her heart skip a beat. "That means—"

"Exactly. We're gonna run out of oxygen." Stan breathed deeply. "Not to mention that the lantern isn't helping. It's burning up our air. So, unless you have a nail file able to dig a hole through this marble, we're dead," he said, slapping the surface. "Yeah, and it's only, like, a foot thick."

Jodi hadn't factored in the possibility of suffocation. She sipped another breath. *Dear Jesus—no. Not that!* she thought. The words *My grace is sufficient* echoed in her mind.

Stan spat. "Me? I say God put us here to die. So curse him, and get it over with."

Funny, that's the same thing Job's friends said to him when he lost everything, Jodi thought. She opened her mouth to make a point when a cockroach scampered between them. Jodi nearly jumped out of her skin. "Stan!"

He smacked the bug with his fist, then picked it up by a leg. "You want it, or may I enjoy the snack?" Stan said, dangling the insect above his mouth.

Jodi leaned away from him. "Ooh, you're sick."

"Hey, we're talking serious protein."

"How gross—"

"I hear they're not so bad with catsup."

She punched him in the leg, then surveyed the floor for other invaders.

Several minutes passed in a hushed silence. She never heard a silence so perfectly devoid of sound.

"Stan?"

"What?"

"This is gonna sound crazy."

"Try me."

She raked her hair. "See, I've never been to a prom. And, uh, it's pretty clear I may never have the chance in, like, the . . . *future.*" Her voice tripped over the word. "Anyway, what I mean to say is, would you, like, dance with me?"

"Huh?"

"It's prom night and, well, we're kinda dressed up," she said, shaking out the filth from her skirt. "The only thing missing is music. But we could sort of imagine that part."

He leaned his head against the hard surface of the wall and closed his eyes, still breathing heavily. "I can't believe we're having this conversation."

She blushed. "It's not like I asked you to feed a shark."

"Jodi, give me a break here—"

"What? You'd rather talk about your dumb sports and just pretend we're not two feet from a dead body?"

"No, but why do we have to talk about . . ." His voice trailed off.

"About death? It happens to everyone," she said. She set Heather's purse on the ground, stood, and walked to the casket, which rested on a three-foot-high pedestal. With several swipes of her hand in the center of the lid on top of the casket, she dusted off the name plate.

"We all end up like"—she squinted—"like Fred Barnes here. Unless you have some magic plan." Jodi swallowed hard. "Our time happens to be now. So, I say, how about a last dance?"

Stan looked up at her, searching her eyes. "You're so . . . so not freaked. How come?"

She pulled her hair back. "I guess I haven't ruled out God, that's all," she said. "I, uh, believe he can find a way—even from a grave." She extended a hand to Stan. "He did it once before, you know."

Stan gazed at her for a long moment, wiped his hand on his pants, then placed it in hers. He stood and gently drew her to himself. They danced, slowly, in a circle. For a long, quiet moment, the walls of the tomb melted away. She could hear the beating of Stan's heart. She could smell a trace of his aftershave. She drew comfort from his strong arms. She felt as if she could dance forever.

"Kind of like Romeo and Juliet, huh?" Stan offered.

"Shh. You're ruining the music," Jodi said, her eyes closed. And while she enjoyed the moment, she wondered what it would feel like to be truly in love with a man. To be kissed by the one you loved. To share in the private laugher couples embraced.

"This is nuts," Stan began. "Heck, if only we had a cell phone, or maybe—"

"Shh!" Jodi put a finger to his lips.

In the stillness that followed, Stan tucked his arm halfway around her waist. "Where'd you learn to—"

"Shut up, Stan. Didn't you hear that?"

"Hear what?"

Jodi froze. "It's, like, a baby's rattle."

"You're losing it, Jodi." He attempted to dance.

She swatted him. "Maybe, but I know what I heard. Would you just stop and listen . . . there . . . Hear it? There it is again." She took a half step back from Stan to peer into the dark corners. Just behind them, she thought she saw a pair of cat's eyes staring back at her.

"What is it, Jodi?"

"Sta-an . . . oh my *gosh* . . ." Her face burned red hot, as if scorched by the sun. She sank her fingers into Stan's arm.

He followed her gaze. "Is that what I think—" Stan didn't bother finishing his question.

The seven-foot-wide coffin was the highest, and only, safe spot out of the snake's deadly reach. Stan dived for the top of the casket, leaving Jodi in its path.

Jodi felt the walls closing in. "Help me, Stan! It's coming at me—"

His massive arms lifted her up. The snake struck at her leg, missing by a breath. She struggled to balance on the curved casing. With each movement, her bruised ribs stabbed like knives against her lungs.

"How'd that get in here?"

"Elvis," Jodi said, panting like a winded dog.

"You mean—"

Jodi, still attempting to pull in enough usable air, nodded. "Yeah, I saw him put something in here. I couldn't tell what it was then, but that looks to me like a timber rattlesnake."

The reptile slithered into the open. Its scales, a patchwork of fear-producing colors, were woven down the length of its four-foot body.

Stan tucked his legs underneath him. "How can you be so sure that's a whatever?"

"Biology," Jodi said. Her heart pounded out of control. "I . . . I did a paper. There's, like, three poisonous snakes in Pennsylvania—"

"Poisonous?"

"Yeah—"

"Like, how poisonous?"

"As in deadly."

The snake's flattened head bobbed, as if in agreement. Its rattle louder now, Jodi half expected it to crawl up and sink its fangs in them.

"That's not a copperhead or a massasauga," she said, wishing she had a club. She leaned forward to be sure, and almost slipped from the safety of their roost.

"Watch it!" Stan yelled, grabbing her by the waist.

"I'm okay, thanks," Jodi said, repositioning herself.

They fell silent.

Stan spoke next. "This is so un-freaking-believably whacked. If we don't suffocate first, the snake will get us."

Jodi shook her head. "Maybe not."

"Jodi, don't tell me you still believe in miracles," Stan said, smacking the casket with a fist. "I sure don't."

CHAPTER 27 ✦ FRIDAY, 7:55 P.M.

Agent Nick Steele unrolled a three-by-four-foot map of the Valley Forge area across his desk. He leaned forward, arms outstretched, hands resting on the desktop, palms down. His eyes darted across the landscape. Like a general going to war, he reviewed a possible plan of attack.

Nick spoke to the map. "Where are you taking them, Billy?"

A minute later, Dwayne, Frank, and Steve entered the room. The agents stood at the edge of the nerve center.

"You wanted to see us?" Dwayne said.

Nick didn't look up. "Dwayne?"

"Sir?"

Nick smoothed the map with the flat side of his hands. "Ever play Where's Waldo?"

"Can't say that I have, sir."

"I have, and I always find him." Nick looked Dwayne, Frank, and Steve in the eyes. "Tonight is no different. We *will* nail Billy Bender. Understood?"

Nods all around.

"Let's get started," Nick said. "Valley Forge is here. As you can see, it's surrounded primarily by a residential area and a few parks. Very little industrial activity. I can't imagine the point of taking them to a residential spot—doesn't fit the dance theme."

"What about the King of Prussia mall," Dwayne suggested, pointing due east. "It's close to Valley Forge. Would he take them there?"

Nick shook his head. "I'd rule that out. Why take them to the mall out there when the Willow Grove Mall would have been much closer?"

"Right."

"I'm thinking secluded areas," Nick said. He jammed a finger down on the map. "You got the Lower Perkiomen Valley Park just north. Mill Road Park to the south. A small city park to the east."

Frank said, "Yeah, and there are—what?—three or four country clubs all around it. That's a bunch of turf, boss."

Nick placed an unlit cigar in his mouth. "Boys, let's not forget the Valley Forge National Park is two thousand–plus acres of grass and trees."

The men surveyed the map in silence.

Steve said, "Looks like the Schuylkill River cuts through the top third of the park. You think he's gonna drown them?"

Nick was weighing the thought when his private phone purred. "Give me a minute alone." They filed out as Nick reached for the phone. He snatched it up sharply. "Yes?"

"I've been thinking," Jake started.

"Smart man."

"Yeah, well, I've been thinking I'd sleep a whole lot better if I knew the deal was on."

"I'm busy here," Nick said, squeezing the handset. "You got something for me, then spit it out."

"A funny thing happened the other day."

Nick held his tongue.

"Get this. My daughter stopped by to see me, man," Jake said. "First time in two years."

"Fifteen seconds, Jake, and I'm hanging up."

"Don't be stupid with me." Jake paused. "I'm trying to say she looked all grown up. Kinda got me thinking about those kids tonight . . . What Billy's doing ain't right, see?"

"Five seconds."

Jake coughed. "He's taking them to the Washington Memorial Gardens . . . It's a cemetery."

Nick scribbled a note. "Anything else?"

"Ain't that enough? It's all I got."

"I'll do what I can for you, Jake. That I promise."

"Yeah, right. I wasn't born yesterday," Jake said. "Just so you know. I told him I had a mole inside the FBI, you know, to save face. At least don't let him know I squealed."

Nick nodded. "I won't. Jake, you did the right thing."

"Whatever."

A harsh click sounded in Nick's ear. He punched the speaker phone. "Dwayne, get in here."

His door flew open. Dwayne, Frank, and Steve bounded to his desk. "What's the word?" Dwayne asked.

Nick devoured the map. "I got a hot tip. Says he's taking them . . . here . . . to the Washington Memorial Gardens. I want you to request backup from the local PDs in Phoenixville, Chester Springs, Audubon, King of Prussia, and Devon."

"Done."

"I want to seal off that cemetery—here, and here." Nick circled the spots with a marker. "I want blockades on the secondary roads leading to the Gardens here, here, and here. Cut off all access to the area."

"We'll shut it down, sir," Dwayne said. "What about dogs? With those woods, the perp may run."

"Good. Make it happen." Nick rolled his sleeves up to his elbows. "I want the chopper and your agents, armed, ready to leave in five minutes."

"What about paramedics?" Dwayne asked. "You want a Medevac on standby?"

"Do it." Nick raised a finger. "One more thing. Give my cell number to Mr. Adams in case he has any contact with his daughter. Now go."

The agents vanished in a flurry of activity.

Alone, Nick reached into his pocket and withdrew a key ring. With it, he unlocked the lower left drawer of his desk and withdrew a newly issued M26 Taser stun gun. Just seven thousand were in service nationwide. He knew its range of twenty-one feet would keep him safely out of the lethal zone during a counterattack. And the laser sent to the target prior to firing assured accuracy. Especially in the dark.

The high-voltage electric shock would do the rest.

Jodi watched the rattlesnake worm its way closer. A thin, red forked tongue darted in and out of its mouth, as if anticipating a tasty morsel. Was it her imagination, or was the snake growing longer by the minute? She longed to be free of this place. If only the door would magically swing open.

On the off-chance that the door cooperated with her dream, she knew she wouldn't be able to move, at least not for a while. Her legs, tucked beside her, were paralyzed with numbness from sitting atop the casket.

Each breath she took taxed her lungs. She guessed the level of oxygen inside the vault was getting dangerously low. Maybe Stan was right. Maybe God wasn't going to provide a way out after all.

As if reading her mind, Stan leaned toward her. "Where's your God now?"

Jodi shrugged. "Honestly? I'm clueless."

"So," Stan said, squeezing the back of his neck, "like I said, if God's so good, what's with dumping us here to rot?"

Jodi coughed up a dust ball. "I'll tell you something, Stan. I don't believe in God just because everything, like, always works out." She put a hand on his shoulder. "Plenty of things don't go my way. Happens all the time. But I still trust him."

"That's nuts. Why bother believing?"

"You want, like, the short or long answer?"

"The short." He leaned his head back against the wall.

"God isn't Santa Claus, or some genie that grants my wishes, you know, if rubbed the right way."

"Then why—"

"I'm not sure if this makes sense," she said. "But, like, I trust him for what he's *already* done for me." Jodi used a finger to draw a small cross on the surface of the dusty casket. "Didn't you look up that verse you used on your fake Web site?"

Stan blushed. "You mean that John 3:16 deal?"

"Bingo."

"Well, not exactly," Stan said. "I only picked it because I always see some guy at football games holding up a sign with it. I figured it must be popular or something."

Jodi closed her eyes and then recited the verse from memory. "'For God so loved the world that he gave his one and only Son, that whoever believes in him shall not perish but have eternal life.'" She opened her eyes. "You know something, Stan? That was the first verse I learned."

"I'm touched—"

She punched his leg. "You can be such a jerk sometimes, Stan."

"Yeah, well, forgive me, but I'm kinda more worked up over the lack of air than all that eternity stuff." He wiped his forehead with the back of his hand. "And your Jesus talk is giving me a headache."

Jodi looked away, and then glanced down. She followed the snake with her eyes as it glided toward Heather's purse. *Lord, please, let Stan somehow see you're really here.*

The purse.

"What is it, Lord?" Jodi said, just above a whisper.

"You talking to me?" Stan said sarcastically.

"That's it!" Jodi said with a clap. "Thank you, Jesus!"

"That's what?" Stan's head jerked forward. "And what's with the brain-dead revival service?"

"Stan, you'll never believe what I just remembered." Jodi's head oscillated between looking at Stan and looking at the purse. "Heather has one of those Instant Messenger thingies in there. At least, I'm pretty sure about that."

"I don't understand how—"

"Now who's dense?" Jodi pulled her hair back. "We can send an e-mail, or better, an IM to somebody and ask for help. Get it?"

"Gosh, you're right. I get it." A wide smile filled his face.

"Now, Stan, be careful when you go to get the purse—"

"Excuse me? I don't recall volunteering."

"I thought you were Stan, 'da Man,'" Jodi said, with an elbow. "Maybe I got you confused with Indiana Jones. C'mon, Stan. I've got a few broken ribs here, otherwise I'd play the hero."

Stan leaned forward and pointed to the snake. "What about Mr. Poison Face?"

"Throw something at it," Jodi said. She could feel the blood circulating to her legs once again.

"Like what?"

"Your shoe . . . anything to distract it."

"Negative. You throw a sandal since I'm doing the running."

Jodi scrunched her nose. Stan was right. She peeled off a sandal, reluctant to let go of it, but at the same time knowing she was out of options. "Ready?"

"Wait until I give you the signal." He lowered himself to the floor as slowly as possible and then took three tentative steps toward the center of the room. "Now!"

The toss landed a foot to the right of the snake. With a snap, mouth wide open revealing the pinkish interior, it wasted no time striking at the threat. Although Jodi was sitting high above the action, she drew back.

Stan, for his part, dashed to the purse. Years of doing sprints at football practice paid off. He grabbed it as if he had recovered a fumbled ball, then rushed the three yards back to the casket. He was halfway up when Jodi noticed the snake had lost interest in the sandal and was slithering with surprising speed toward Stan.

"Stan! Jump!"

He tossed her the purse in order to pull himself up the five feet with both arms. She clung to the strap, knowing her life depended on it. A second later, Jodi's jaw came unhinged.

Stan cried out, "Oh, God, it's got me!"

Jodi's blood froze. The snake's mouth was wrapped around the back side of Stan's shoe. "Oh my gosh. Shake it off!"

Stan kicked off the loafer and the snake dropped to the floor. He pulled himself to the top, then tore his sock off. He was sweating as if he had just competed in the Super Bowl. Bending his ankle, he studied his heel. "What's that look like to you, Jodi?"

Jodi was almost too shocked to speak.

"C'mon. What do you see?" Stan said, his voice cracking.

"You've been scratched and, uh, it's pretty deep." With her left hand, she hooked her hair around her ear. "Listen to me. That doesn't mean he had a chance to—" She wanted to sound positive, but her voice betrayed her.

"Oh, God, I'm going to die!"

Her heart almost broke in half as tears rolled down Stan's face.

"Please hurry with that thing," Stan said, then closed his eyes and leaned his head back. "My ankle feels kinda numb."

Jodi commanded her hands to open the purse.

"Got it." Her hands trembled as she opened the Instant Messenger. She powered it up, then attempted to sign on using the guest feature and her screen name. She typed her password, pushed the SIGN ON button, and then waited for the connection. She prayed the signal would find its way through the marble walls.

Ten seconds later, she shouted, "Yes!" The signal was weak, but she was in cyberspace. Fifteen seconds passed, then an angry beep sounded. She angled the two-inch screen toward the light for better viewing. She read the display in complete disbelief: *Only one screen name per account can be on-line at a time.*

Jodi's heart sank. She struggled to breathe. Her dad or mom must be tying up the account.

"I can't sign on."

Stan moaned. "Why not?"

"I guess my parents are on," she said, blowing her bangs with an upward breath. "And I can't use Kat's screen name. I don't know her password."

"Use mine—"

"Awesome." Jodi squeezed his arm. "Remind me. What is it?"

"JesusFreakster2," he said, his lips turning blue.

Jodi strained to key the information in the space marked GUEST SIGN-IN. With one finger on the tiny keyboard, she almost dropped the device. The backside of her eyes throbbed. "What's your password?"

"Not supposed to give that out—"

"Duh, I think this counts as an emergency."

"I'd rather not—"

"You're delirious, Stan. You can't even see straight. Don't waste time."

He coughed, then inhaled a raspy breath. "ILvLucy."

The edges of her mouth curled into a smile as she worked the keyboard. She remembered Stan was a closet *I Love Lucy Show* fan. A handful of seconds later, she was on.

"Okay, Heather, please be there." From the moment Jodi discovered the Instant Messenger, she had prayed Heather would realize they might use it to communicate. She knew there was no way Heather and Kat would go to dinner, or the prom for that matter. Not with them missing.

A friendly chime sounded, indicating Jodi had received a knock-knock. She just about fainted.

IluvHim4Ever2:	Stan?
JesusFreakster2:	Its Jodi SOS!
IluvHim4Ever2:	Where's Stan?
JesusFreakster2:	W/me really sick
IluvHim4Ever2:	How do I know it's u?

Jodi grinned. Looked like Heather was learning.

JesusFreakster2:	Ask a question
IluvHim4Ever2:	Where were u 2 weeks ago on Sat?

Jodi stared at the screen. Two weeks ago? "How do I know?" Jodi said under her breath. It was such a blur. *Gosh, how am I supposed to know that? I can't even remember what I had for breakfast,* she thought. She was about to ask for a different question when the memory raced into the front of her mind.

JesusFreakster2:	rave w/Bruce
IluvHim4Ever2:	OMG where r u?
JesusFreakster2:	Washington Memorial Gardens
IluvHim4Ever2:	???
JesusFreakster2:	a cemetery / Valley Forge
IluvHim4Ever2:	OMG! OMG! Y?
JesusFreakster2:	snake bite def SOS
IluvHim4Ever2:	where r u near?
JesusFreakster2:	w dead Fred Barnes

A sharp click, followed by the sound of something dragging, registered somewhere on the edge of her ear. She glanced at Stan, his breathing heavy and labored, then back at the screen for Heather's message.

IluvHim4Ever2:	ur dad called FBI
JesusFreakster2:	PTL

A moment later, her nose caught a whiff of fresh air. Her bare arms registered a faint impression of a breeze, almost as if a window had been opened across town. She looked up and found herself staring at the hooded face of Elvis standing by the door. Her heart zoomed past Mars.

She thought he had left them to die. Now what? More snakes? Nothing made sense. She frantically dashed out a message.

JesusFreakster2:	Im b/ing attack

Elvis took several steps into the tomb, the sound reverberating off the walls. He confronted the snake. With a kick, the snake sailed to the far corner. Jodi heard, but couldn't see, the rattle shaking with provoked intensity. She couldn't miss, however, the masked face shaking with rage a foot from her nose.

"Give that to me!" Elvis said.

He yanked the device away, and then, with the back of his hand, slapped Jodi across the face. Her cheek stung as if attacked by a mob of angry hornets.

Outside the sealed tomb, Billy cursed. He walked to the limousine, slipped inside, then slammed the door so hard, the six-inch TV monitor toppled from the dash to the seat. With his right hand, he snatched the TV and jammed it back in place.

Billy turned over the Instant Messaging device he held in his left hand, examining every side. He had searched her purse, and didn't see it. The blasted thing looked like a compact case. He opened it. The little screen, still active, awaited a response. He read the message and wondered how much she had already communicated, and to whom.

Billy was about to crush the IM device, then changed his mind. *Two can play this game*, he thought.

He'd just send a little message of his own.

IluvHim4Ever2:	u there?
JesusFreakster2:	yup. nm about that stuff. We're ok
IluvHim4Ever2:	????
JesusFreakster2:	def j/k
IluvHim4Ever2:	u sure?
JesusFreakster2:	yup. g2g. cya

Billy snapped the case shut, then eyed his TV monitor. He watched with mixed pleasure as the teens struggled to keep the now-agitated snake from climbing up the pedestal. The four tiny cameras, installed just that afternoon, were doing a remarkable job catching the drama. The lantern provided the perfect ambiance. It should be a hot ticket on the Web site.

Everything was going perfect.

Until now.

He was unsure whether to stay or leave. To leave meant an end to the taping; to stay, he risked discovery. He looked back at the screen in time to see the girl trying to hit the snake with a purse. How wonderfully pathetic. A vicious smile crossed his face. This was too good to pass up.

He'd chance maybe thirty minutes before leaving.

At the hinge, he snapped the Instant Messenger in half.

Nick checked his watch. The helicopter had just passed over a galaxy of twinkling lights thrown off by the King of Prussia mall. He calculated they would arrive at the Washington Memorial Gardens in less than three minutes. For the sake of two teens, he hoped they weren't too late. Nick felt a tap on his shoulder. He turned his head halfway around.

"Sir, I have the groundskeeper on the line," Dwayne said, leaning forward in his jump seat. "Says he was mowing grass just before dark when he spotted a white limousine in the northwestern quadrant of the cemetery. That's over by the tall pines."

Nick, sitting in the right front seat, said, "Pilot, you get that?"

"Roger that. Now heading northwest."

"Can we get that searchlight fired up?" Nick asked.

The pilot flipped a switch and the near-blinding light pierced the darkness below.

Nick smiled. "Hey, Elvis. I got you a spotlight right here. Let's see you start dancing."

"Sir," Dwayne said. "The area has been completely sealed off as per your instructions."

Nick flashed Dwayne a thumbs-up and then studied the terrain below. The high-pitched whine of his cell phone erupted in his shirt pocket. "Agent Steele here."

"Mr. Steele, I'm Jodi's dad, Jack Adams. Sorry to bother—"

"Not at all. How can I help?"

"Two things, but it's a bit confusing. We heard from Jodi a few minutes ago—"

"Yes?"

"She used a friend's Instant Messenger device. Said she was at the Washington Memorial Gardens—"

"I'm on top of that as we speak."

"Well, she said she was inside the tomb of a Fred Barnes, which doesn't make sense—"

"Think mausoleum." Nick turned to Dwayne, cupping the phone, and said, "Ask your caretaker where the vault of Fred Barnes is. Pronto." He spoke into the phone. "Please, continue."

"And, she reported her friend Stan had been attacked by a snake—"

"One second, Mr. Adams." Nick snapped his fingers and Dwayne leaned forward, his ear to a phone. "We need that Medevac—ASAP."

Dwayne nodded.

"Okay, Mr. Adams," Nick said. "What's the confusing part?"

"She said she was being attacked. Then, about a minute later, she denied the whole thing. Said it was all a joke and we shouldn't worry."

Nick leaned his head to the right, looking out the window. No way was this a prank. Too many things lined up. Then again, there was always the possibility, however improbable, that Jake was stringing along the agency as payback for putting him in jail. Was that it?

"Mr. Steele?"

Nick cleared his throat. "Does your daughter have a habit of pulling elaborate pranks?"

"Well, no, actually."

"Then don't believe this is just a joke. Listen to me, Mr. Adams. I assure you we're doing everything possible to get her back safely—"

The edge of the spotlight glinted off a metal object. The brief reflection of light bounced skyward, catching the corner of Nick's eye. A chrome bumper. "I'm sorry. I've got to go. We'll talk." Nick folded his cell phone and stuffed it in his pocket while barking out an order.

"There—to the left. Circle back—that's our man."

Billy heard the approach of the helicopter long before the chopper's searchlight punctured the darkness. At the sight of the brilliant light sweeping circles in his direction, he felt a tightness, like the preamble to a heart attack, spread throughout his chest. His interest in the TV monitor was replaced by this new, unwelcome development.

While his instincts told him this was the FBI, he fought the temptation to jump to conclusions. There were, after all, any number of other reasonable explanations for the unexpected aircraft. Maybe it was the Discovery Channel filming a piece on historic national cemeteries; a producer from the local TV news doing a feature story on graveyard vandalism; or the police searching for an escaped criminal or lost child.

Maybe.

More likely, the Feds had tracked him here just as they had tracked him to the RV park.

There was no way to know for sure.

Billy had seconds to make a move. He quickly assessed the possibilities. Assuming the worst—that the FBI was hovering overhead—he knew he couldn't outrun them on foot. Not with a bad leg. He couldn't outrace them with a vehicle as cumbersome as the limousine. He couldn't outshoot them with just a handgun. And he wasn't sure he could outsmart them.

There simply wasn't enough time to plan.

He watched as the helicopter touched down twenty yards in front of him. It blocked the access road. He reached across the seat for his chauffeur's hat, placed it on his head, then pulled the pistol from inside his shoulder harness. He kept the weapon low and out of sight in the off-chance he didn't need to use it.

He watched the doors of the helicopter open and six men deplane, three on each side. The men, silhouetted by the aircraft's landing lights, fanned out and took up positions around the perimeter of the limousine. Each carried high-powered rifles.

Billy ruled out the Discovery Channel.

An older man with a bald head, Billy noticed, approached his side of the car, yet remained a dozen yards away.

Billy lowered the window.

"Is there a problem, sir?" He adjusted his chauffeur's hat as he spoke, pretending to be unfazed by the presence of the posse.

"FBI," the bald man said. "I need you to slowly step out of the vehicle. Put your hands on the hood of the car."

"Listen, about the trespassing thing," Billy began. "I realize we're not supposed to be here, but, hey, I'm just doing my job, see." Billy rested his left elbow on the window frame. "The couple wanted to grab a lip lock, if you know what I mean. Heck, I say it's sick, being in a cemetery and all. Kids these days—who knows how they get this way."

The agent assumed the stance of a shooter, legs spread, hands raised in front. He aimed a small handgun at Billy. Two seconds later, Billy saw a red dot appear on his shoulder. He tightened his grip around the Glock in his right hand, inching it onto his lap. Thick drops of sweat rolled down his back.

"Sir, I repeat, step out of the car."

Billy slipped his left hand into his inner jacket and retrieved his driver's license. He held it out the window. "I'm telling you, there must be some kind of misunderstanding. Here's my license."

"C'mon, Billy. It's over."

At the sound of his name, a cold fear burned in his gut. He pictured Jake. The orange prison jumpsuit. The assigned prisoner number stamped on the pocket. The ankle chains. The barbed wire. The armed guards . . . and Dutch.

No way. Not him.

Billy swallowed hard.

He pressed the Glock against his chest.

"You're right," Billy said. "It's over." He squeezed the trigger, then slumped forward against the horn.

CHAPTER 31 ✳ FRIDAY, 9:01 P.M.

Jodi dabbed at Stan's forehead with a tissue from Heather's purse. His skin, hot to the touch, dripped with sweat. As she worked, she glanced at Stan's heel. It had started to swell about the same time he had complained of a rubbery taste in his mouth. Both, she knew, were signs the snake did more than break his skin. She wanted to rinse out the bite and would gladly pay any amount for a bar of soap and a cup of water.

She didn't know how fast the venom would kill a big guy like Stan. She knew he had longer to live than a few minutes, but probably less than a few hours. Was the FBI really on the way? Would they even be able to find the tomb in the dark?

Dear God, let them get here in time.

"Stan, listen to me."

Like a window shade, his eyelids rolled up halfway.

"Hang on, help *is* coming," Jodi said. "I promise, you're gonna be okay." She managed a smile, although, with the snake still patrolling the space just below them and the lantern about to burn out above them, she wasn't so sure.

"I . . . I feel so . . . cold," Stan said.

"Here," Jodi said, tearing a two-inch-wide strip of fabric from the hem of her skirt. "Give me your ankle." She loosely wrapped the makeshift bandage three inches above the bite area, making sure she could still slip a finger under it. "I read somewhere that should slow the venom."

If only she could do something to stop that endless rattling. Even though timber rattlesnakes were a protected species, she promised herself she would kill the snake if given both the chance and, oh, maybe a rocket launcher.

Another thing bothered her. She could go a month without food. Three days without water. But, she couldn't go more than a day without sleep. And, given that she was exhausted, she had to consider the prospect of sleeping while sitting on top of a casket. What if she fell off? What if she woke up and discovered the snake in her lap, just inches from her face?

She closed and then rubbed her eyes, yawning. When she opened them, she blinked twice in disbelief. The room was completely devoid of light. Seconds later, she smelled the charred end of the lantern's smoldering wick.

Perfect. Now what?

At least one thing was positive. Breathing was easier ever since Elvis stormed in and took the Instant Messenger. She figured the oxygen level must have been partially replenished when the door opened. Count your blessings, right?

That's odd, she thought. *How did he know I had it?* It's not like the creep had x-ray vision. Or did he?

As before, she heard the door opening with a click and a dragging sound. Elvis must have seen the light go out. On instinct, she drew her knees to her chest, and a hand to her face, bracing herself for his next assault.

She started to pray silently. *Please, Jesus—*

An unfamiliar voice called out. "Jodi Adams, Stan Taylor, are you in there? I'm with the FBI." She saw a powerful flashlight cut through the floating dust.

Her pounding heart got in the way of her vocal cords. She tried to say, "We're over here!" but the words failed to come.

Jodi saw the reptile recoil, ready to launch at the new source of light. She cleared the debris from her throat and then choked out, "Watch the snake!"

The flash of red light was followed by a sharp popping sound. Although she couldn't see what hit the snake, the effect was immediate.

The beast thrashed left, then right, whipping its rattle into an angry fit. With a twitch, it flopped belly up and ceased to move.

"We're clear," came the comforting voice. A tall, bald man entered the room. "Jodi, I'm Nick Steele. I presume this is Stan. Where was he bitten?"

"On the right heel. Please, hurry," Jodi said.

Nick called over his shoulder, "I need the EMT, pronto."

Two emergency medical technicians raced through the door. Aided by the flashlight, they arranged Stan on a stretcher, strapped him in place, and then hooked him up to an IV bag.

As they worked to stabilize Stan, Jodi lowered herself down from the casket. Her legs almost buckled.

Nick said, "Here, let me give you a hand."

Jodi took his arm. "Thanks. I'm so glad you're here."

After the paramedics carried Stan from the tomb, Jodi walked in silence with Nick through the door. She paused beside the two stone lions. She looked to the stars and then whispered, *"Thank you, Jesus."* A fresh supply of tears washed her eyes.

"Are you all right, Jodi?" Nick said.

She nodded, without wiping away the tears, then followed him away from the tomb. "What happened to Elvis?"

"His real name was Billy Bender—"

"Was?" Jodi said. She watched the workers remove his body from the car.

Nick led her past the limousine toward the helicopter. "I would have preferred to have taken his sorry butt in," Nick said. He threw his cigar to the ground, squishing it with his heel. "I'm afraid he took the coward's way out."

Jodi, wrapped in a terry robe, lingered by the kitchen bay window. Baptized by the early morning sun, her face glowed. She breathed a slow, cleansing breath, savoring the warmth and brilliance of the new day. She rested a hand on the windowpane.

Heather appeared at her side. "You're up early. Couldn't you sleep?"

"Are you kidding?" Jodi said, still gazing outside. "Last night, sitting on Fred's casket, I thought I'd never see a sunrise again." She looked at Heather. "How could I miss it today?"

Heather looked down. "You know, this is all my fault."

"Is that what you think?"

"Of course it is," Heather said. "It wouldn't have happened if I wasn't, like, trying to meet some dream guy on-line." She looked up. "From now on, I'm only using the phone—"

"Will you knock it off," Jodi said. "Just be, like, super careful."

"And, what about that Elvis guy?" Heather squeezed Jodi's arm. "Oh, my gosh, Jodi, I would've been so freaked—"

"Hey, let's not talk about it just yet," Jodi said. "I'm still trying to, like—"

The wall-mounted kitchen phone rang. Heather, standing between Jodi and the phone, snatched up the handset. "Hello? Adams family."

Jodi whispered, "I hate it when you say that."

Heather covered the mouthpiece and with a wink said, "I know." She listened. "Sure. One second." Heather extended the phone to Jodi. "Says he's some guy named Billy Bender."

Jodi froze. Billy was dead, wasn't he? For a split second, she relived the whole nightmare. She feared the snake would scoot out from under the kitchen table.

"Hello?"

Three seconds of heavy breathing steamed up the phone line.

An affected voice spoke. "Jodi. Remember me? It's Billy."

"STAN! Where are you?"

"I'm still at the hospital. Oh, and the doc says I'm gonna be fine. Why?"

"Wait 'til I get my hands on you. I'm gonna—"

"Whoa!" he said, laughing. "Is that a Christian thing to do?"

Jodi rolled her eyes. "And what do you know about that?"

"You'd be surprised."

"Meaning what?"

"Meaning I've been, like, watching you, Jodi."

"Yeah, you and Billy both," she said.

Stan laughed. "C'mon, Jodi. I'm actually trying to be serious."

Jodi rested the phone on her shoulder, then started to preen the ends of her hair. "Okay—go."

"Well, like, last night I couldn't sleep. I kept thinking about how we almost—"

"Died," Jodi said.

"Exactly." Stan coughed. "I mean, c'mon. It's not every day you get carried out of a tomb for a second chance, you know?"

"I totally understand," Jodi said.

"And," Stan continued, "Jodi, you seemed so at peace with the fact we were gonna die. Not me. I was so mad and afraid. Gosh, I don't want to live that way."

Jodi felt her eyes moisten around the edges. "What are you saying, Stan?"

"You know how I, like, pretended to be a Christian with that bogus Web page and that whole JesusFreakster2 thing?"

She switched the phone to the other ear. "Yeah."

"Well, it's time I stopped pretending—and let's just say, I called because I could use a little coaching."

Jodi looked at Heather, eyes wide open, then cupped the phone with her hand. "Stan wants to become a Christian—wake up Kat and start praying."

Heather squeezed Jodi's arm, then dashed down the stairs.

Jodi took a deep breath. "Stan, how about this: Why don't I say a prayer, and you can sort of pray along in your heart?"

"Sounds good."

"Okay." Jodi pulled the barstool out and then sat down. "Well, dear Jesus, I need you now. I know that my sin keeps me from you. But because you loved me, you took my place by dying on the cross. Please come into my heart and change me. In Jesus' name, amen."

"Amen," Stan said. "So how does this work? Is it my turn?"

"Uh-huh."

"All right, then," Stan said. "Um, Jesus, I agree with everything Jodi said. Plus I, um, thank you for friends like Jodi who are patient with guys like me. Help me to become that kind of, um, team player to others. Amen."

Jodi swiped three napkins from the counter to dry her tears.

THE AUTHORS WOULD LIKE TO EXTEND
THEIR APPRECIATION TO:

Carissa DeMoss, Leticia DeMoss, Robert and Dora DeMoss, Cy Fenton, Greg Johnson, Ami McConnell, Olivia Paoletti, Jeff Parrish, and Rebecca Wilson.

Special thanks to Robby Gilreath and the team at the Residence Inn, Brentwood, Tennessee.

In the tradition of MTV's *The Real World*, eight high-school juniors volunteer for a week on a houseboat in the name of experimental education. Rosie Meyer, the former Olympic silver medalist turned social studies teacher, dreams of her students learning firsthand the realities of tolerance and diversity. And learn they do. The issues faced, the truths uncovered, and the lessons learned leave them changed for a lifetime.

It's Labor Day weekend—and more than 15,000 ravers have gathered for a 72-hour dance party in a waterfront warehouse in Philadelphia. Kat is strung out on drugs and next to her lies the body of a dead boy. Jodi wants answers—and justice. How did the boy die? Is Kat next? And why have the police refused to help? Nothing can prepare Jodi for the fact that some kids are worth more dead than alive.

W PUBLISHING GROUP™
www.wpublishinggroup.com